I0637869

Out of the Gutter
And into His Grace

By

J. Renée

J. Renee Henry. © 2019

All rights reserved. No part of this book may be reproduced, stored, or transmitted by any means- whether auditory, graphic, mechanical, or electronic- without written permission of both publisher and author, except in the case of brief excerpts used in critical articles and certain other noncommercial uses permitted by copyright law. Unauthorized reproduction of any part of this work is illegal and is punishable by law.

ISBN: 978-0-578-45705-5
For more information, please visit www.lifezanopenbook.com

Because of the dynamic nature of the internet, any web addresses or links contained in this book may have changed since publication and may no longer be valid. The views expressed in this work are solely those of the author and do not necessarily reflect the views of the publisher, and the publisher disclaims any responsibility for them.

Printed in the United States of America

DISCLAIMER: Names, characters, businesses, places, events, locales, and incidents are either the products of the author's imagination or used in a fictitious manner. Any resemblance to actual persons, living or dead, or actual events is purely coincidental.

𝔇𝔢𝔡𝔦𝔠𝔞𝔱𝔦𝔬𝔫

I dedicate this book to my mother, my real "Honey" Louisa Battle-Henry. The little lady in stature with the huge heart. The lady who taught me to stand on my own and never be afraid to speak up for myself. She taught me how to be courageous in the face of adversity. There are no giants in my world that I can't stand up to.

Table Of Contents

Acknowledgments..vii

Chapter 1: Our Humble Beginnings 1

Chapter 2: Moving On 6

Chapter 3: Neighbors 10

Chapter 4: The Raging Bull 17

Chapter 5: The Perfect Gentlemen 19

Chapter 6: Moving on Up 23

Chapter 7: My First Diamond..27

Chapter 8: Faith...29

Chapter 9: Me Too...34

Chapter 10: My Ride or Die 40

Chapter 11: Raising Nick 46

Chapter 12: History of a Harlot.....................................55

Chapter 13: The Silent Cries of the Innocent...............60

Chapter 14: The Fall of the Family................................65

Chapter 15: Ophelia...71

Chapter 16: No More Free Milk.....................................84

Chapter 17: No Winners in this Game...........................93

Chapter 18: I Quit..97

Chapter 19: 90-Day Eviction Notice 100

Chapter 20: A Night to Remember 103

Chapter 21: Out of the Frying Pan 107

Chapter 22: Paving Our Way 113

Chapter 23: From the Palace to the Pigpen 117

Chapter 24: From Bad to Worse 122

Chapter 25: Escaping the Jungle 127

Chapter 26: Praise Tabernacle 130

Chapter 27: Wolves in Sheep's Clothing 135

Chapter 28: Finding My Way into His Grace 144

Epilogue 154

About The Author 155

Contact Information 157

---·❖·---

Acknowledgments

In the early nineties I became inspired by Terry McMillian after reading "Waiting to Exhale" and "Disappearing Acts." I dreamed that I too could someday write a book. However, in between, procrastination and raising four children as a single parent my dreams faded.

As God would have it in March 2018, I attended an event hosted by Teri Williams, "Ladies in Black" where I had the pleasure of being re-acquainted with author and editor Pauline W. Mansfield (The Turtle Queen). In the midst of her speaking it was laid upon her heart to assist me in completing my book, something I'd shared with her many years ago. She offered her services as a writing coach. Thank you for igniting something in me to begin writing again.

Thank you to my children, grandchildren and great grandchildren. Truly if it wasn't for all of you, I would have no desire to pursue my dreams and ALWAYS strive to become a better me, someone you can be proud of. KaMia, Jamaal, Derrick, Justin, Keandré, KaMara, Kristopher, Reign, Jamaal Jr., Journey, Lyriq, Ava, Adriana and Keandré Jr., what a joy it is to have all of you. My life has been enriched because of you.

What a sisterhood God has allowed me to be a part of. I'm so grateful for my "Ride or Dies." I cannot list what each of you have done for me individually because that would be another book. I'll just thank you collectively for all of your support, late night chats, tears, laughter, joys, sorrows, encouragement, motivation and for just believing in me. Theldoshia Rose Green, Gwendolyn Barber-Williams, ChéLonda Byrd-Thomas, Rhudeshia Jones-Crawford, Sheila Graves-Royster, Marcia Mack, Dawn Grimsley, ChéLine Byrd, Ann Riggins, Nicole Satcher, Cathy Walker and Deborah Martin, who is no longer here on earth, but forever in my heart.

A special thank you to a woman I'm unable to describe, Arline Amison. Thank you for teaching me unknowingly the real definition of forgiveness and unconditional love. When God created you, He truly broke the mold.

And to anyone I may have forgotten to list individually, thank you. You know who you are.

Chapter 1

❖

Our Humble Beginnings

As I sat in my room staring out of the window, even the bright sun shining through could not add light to the gloom I was feeling inside. Rumor had it that my high-school sweetheart was planning to take someone else to the prom. How could he? She wasn't even cute! Her knees knocked together like 'Click Clacks', her afro looked like she stuck her finger in a socket, and she was so black she made 'Buckwheat' look light-skin! What did she have that I didn't? *I wanted to die...*

Tommy, the most recognized football player on our team, was 6ft., 175 lbs., and had the sexiest puppy dog brown eyes I'd ever seen. Unlike most of his peers, he even had his own car! -- a 1969 Chevy Impala and I, Kamara Hemphill got to ride shotgun most of the time -- and now, somebody thinks they're taking my spot? *Hell no!* I'm not about to just cross my legs that I had uncrossed many times for him and let that happen! After all, it was me who screamed number 85 from the sidelines on those bitter cold days in Newark, New Jersey. Shouldn't that count for something? Yeah, it should have counted for something, but it didn't count for anything! He was done, moved on taking pieces of my heart with him. I cried, I moped, I called, I got hung up on; I even pretended to go to school, and after my mother left for work I would circle back home. I didn't give a damn about school! It was pure torture to see him walking the halls of Barringer High with her on his arm. I couldn't shake this feeling. I didn't know how to handle this at 17. My Mom took me to a therapist, and he did what they do best - gave me a prescription. I started popping valium, hoping this would help me get over this teenage crush that I called love. Cloud 9 was what I would be on once the drugs started taking effect. I buried my head under my pillow and allowed my mind to drift to a happy place somewhere in between fantasy and reality.

I was 10 years old -- long before any of this heartbreak stuff invaded my heart. We were moving from our home in Poughkeepsie, New York, the Smith Street projects, where the scenery was beautiful and most of our neighbors were family. To someone else, they could have very well been shacks, but they were filled with love and laughter. We never had to lock our doors, we loved and respected each other; so, to us kids nothing else mattered. We didn't know our parents were struggling and we lived in low-income housing.

My dad was called "Big Cheese" by his buddies for reasons unbeknownst to me. It certainly wasn't because he was walking around with bulging pockets. However, my dad worked two jobs to provide for us – one at a big firm called IBM full-time, and as a school bus driver part-time. He would even secure a third seasonal job at Montgomery Ward department store to ensure my sister and I had every gift on our Christmas list. One day, overhearing some grown folks chatter, I learned his nickname derived from his huge smile -- the kind a photographer hopes to capture just before he snaps your picture. My daddy was such a loving, mild-mannered, laid-back human being. You might not have known he was in the room unless he was telling a joke or trying to get everyone to laugh. Perhaps being the total opposite of my mother was what attracted him to her. She, on the other hand, was able to command any room just by walking in. Our parents came from different backgrounds. My mom's family was dysfunctional, and my dad's family appeared to have it all together. Kyndra would inherit our daddy's infectious smile. There were times I thought I had it too but was ALWAYS reminded by other family members that I was just like my mother, almost as if that wasn't a good thing. Therefore, our *"Humble Beginnings"* all began with a feisty little lady, "Honey"(our mom) and a humble, hard-working family man, "Big Cheese"(our dad).

My older sister, Kyndra, and I had everything we needed. We never knew we were poor. We felt like part owners of the neighborhood grocery store. The primary owner kept the books – recording the names and amounts of each family's purchase (those who were obviously creditworthy) in his little black and white composition notebook until they could pay. We would just go in, get what our parents had on 'the list', and put it on 'the bill', then just check out like people charge on credit cards. We would stop at Tony's Meat Market on the way home from school and get a cold hot dog or a piece of bologna to snack on – Wow! Those were the good ole days!! It was a life like Andy in Mayberry. Those were days of trust.

I was my mommy's baby; in her eyes, I could do no wrong, but I knew I was the little brat sister Kyndra could have definitely lived without. We sat down for dinner every night as a family after my dad came home from work and I'd use that time to tell every single one of my sister's secrets. It's no wonder why she couldn't stand me! However, our Christmases seemed magical. There would always be family dropping by to see all of our gifts, and there was plenty to eat and drink. Weekends were pretty routine; Saturday's were spent at Big Ma's and Pops, my dad's parent's house on Pershing Ave. My aunts, uncles, and cousins were there too. So much fun. While our parents were getting drunk, we were sneaking in a few drinks ourselves. On Sunday's my dad would take us for rides while telling his stories about growing up on Spackingkill Road. The best part for me was stopping at Brenner's Ice Cream Parlor. Life was good, so I thought. I would later learn a disheveled mind is easily disguised when your family seems perfect. All was not as it appeared in the Hemphill's household.

My sister began to see things falling apart when she was 13 and puffin' on Salem cigarettes like she was a grown up; this was the one thing I'd keep a secret. My dad was not coming home on time for dinner anymore, and my mom just seemed sad or mad. That mad sadness turned into a very dark depression that one day led her to a ledge outside of our 5th floor apartment window.

There she stood, with a blank stare in her eyes. My uncles were in panic - one standing outside, desperately looking up – praying she would not jump. The other was practically hanging out the window, begging her not to jump, trying to convince her that life really was worth living.

I stood there, almost invisible – a helpless 8-year old girl, tears streaming down my face, and snot running out of my nose. In my mind I was screaming! *"Please don't let my mommy fall!"* Yet, in reality, not one word escaped my mouth. I was terrified! As I stood there trembling, my big sister miraculously appeared. She grabbed my hand and wiped my tears, never saying one word. I looked into her eyes and felt a sense of comfort. Her expression was really hard to read – was she disgusted with my mom or was she sad? I knew she had always felt that I was mommy's *"Little Poopie"* and she was the problem teenager. Just a few months before, after our daddy left, I heard my sister tell her best friend that she wished our mother was dead! While I stood there in terror hoping my mommy wouldn't fall (not clearly comprehending she really wanted to jump), my sister was probably thinking, *'hurry up and jump so my daddy can come rescue us — sluts don't deserve to live!!'*

Our once happy household was no longer happy. I'd heard people talk about prayer --if I had known anything about it, now would be the time to do it.

Chapter 2

Moving On

Quickly our fairy tale life ended. My parents separated, and my mom decided it would be best for us to relocate. She packed up, and off we headed to what we called a foreign land. The huge Ryder truck, filled to capacity, moved slowly pass my gang of neighborhood friends waving with tears streaming down their faces as if the truck were a hearse. I cried so hard that day. My life would never be the same. Not only was I losing my friends, but I was also losing my father and my home.

Kyndra was always conservative and glamorous. At a young age she would wear eye shadow and plaster her full lips with lip gloss. She was so pretty. I was just a little skinny girl with a birthmark on my face that I hated! We were as different as day is to night. I always wondered why. Her four friends showed up to see her, off -- one girlfriend and three guys. She was a daddy's girl; she didn't really like my mom anymore since the break-up. Honey wasn't fazed one bit by Kyndra's dislike for her. She moved on, got herself a new man and seemed very happy as a free spirit. I couldn't really fault her she became a mom as a teenager, so now her life was just beginning. There wasn't too much grass growing under daddy's feet either; he was seeing a lady three buildings down who had eight kids and a house that smelled like they mopped their floors with piss! I guess my dad wanted to make sure he got someone who was totally opposite from Honey. Our house was always neat and smelled more like Mr. Clean and lemon scented Pledge.

Honey was making the best decision for her babies by moving us to a new environment. She had developed a reputation with the fellas. In fact, they nicknamed her "The Captain." The talk around town was that we would return one day, but we never did.

Speaking of change...

When we arrived in Newark, New Jersey it was as if we had left Beverly Hills and moved to Harlem. Suddenly we were the average Black family statistic -- a single mom raising two daughters. I had never seen so many Black people during the entire time we lived in Poughkeepsie; our neighborhood was mixed. This whole city seemed to be Black. There would be many adjustments my sister and I would have to make to merely survive in this atmosphere! *What was my mother thinking?!* I knew my grandpa and aunt lived here but did that mean we had to be in this disgusting pit too? In this city, projects were these high-rise brick buildings with torn shades hanging up to some of their windows, broken glass all over the parking lots, and crowds of people just hanging out. The playground had a frame where swings used to be; the kids just hung on the frame as if it was monkey bars. Now our apartment doors not only had to remain locked, but there were chains for extra security and bars on the windows. Was this our new home or were we in prison? Please, can somebody wake me up from this nightmare? I want to go home. This surely didn't feel like home. Leaving Poughkeepsie was one of the saddest times of my life. My mom never allowed us to have pets, but now we had a few who just moved in, no matter how clean she was. We had to learn that Mickey was not only living in Disneyland.

Years passed, and I adjusted. It was a new way of life, and I learned to love it. Just like back in the ole days I made many friends and my sister gained about 4 more. I don't think she ever really adjusted to the city life. However, my Mom was maintaining her charisma with the men. 'The Captain' had found a new place to rule.

Back to reality for me, valium has worn off. I'm too young to be consumed with this heartache, and most importantly I'm not going to be popping pills, staring out of windows like I'm some damn psychopath!

I came home from school one day and there sat a handsome man at our kitchen table sipping on a Budweiser. He smiled, not just any smile but a Taye Diggs kinda smile. Not too much competition for a Black man with nice teeth. I wondered, was this another one of the Captain's fans? He introduced himself as Brother Hakeem (a Muslim). I didn't have to know much about religion to know that he was missing it somewhere, with that can of beer in his hand and the empty shot glass next to it. I found out that his mother occupied the apartment upstairs and he had just stopped down to be cordial to the new neighbors (us). We had upgraded from the apartment on Johnson Avenue, and now we were living in a three-family house on the north side of town. Hakeem visited his mom every day. It later became a habit for him to stop downstairs to visit my mom too. I was still coping with my heartache of having lost Tommy, but I was a lot stronger. I was coming home from school on time which was a rarity. Hakeem was really easy to talk to, so I began seeking advice from him about my failed relationship with Tommy. I learned to trust Hakeem more and more with each counseling session. After several weeks of sulking and writing lovesick poems to the tunes of the saddest Chi-Lites' love songs, I decided I'd cried long enough. It was quite obvious Tommy wasn't coming back. It was also past time for me to get on with my life. After all, seeing Hakeem on a regular basis made me realize that Tommy wasn't as cute as I thought he was. Maybe him and sister 'Click Clacks' deserved each other! Did I fail to mention that in addition to being handsome and very well groomed, Hakeem was outgoing, exciting and he didn't have a curfew! By now he was stopping by for those cordial visits before either of our mothers came home. My ego soared, and at 17, it didn't take much. No doubt, a 25-year-old R. *Kelly* named Hakeem. Hell!, even I believed I could fly!!

No more tears for me over some young, afro wearing, football playing, high school punk with no experience! I would now have my opportunity to bump and grind with a real man, and when that time finally came, I melted like a popsicle on a hot summer day.

Chapter 3

❖

Neighbors

High school ended, and just like that! No more socializing with my peers; no more walking the halls when I should've been in class; no more cheering from the bleachers at the football games, and no more curfews (*as if I had any*). Now, my mornings would be laid back, doing nothing, and my evenings would be turned up with Hakeem.

My high school buddies were making plans for college while I entertained the thought of joining the military. Those thoughts vanished after sitting for damn near six hours in an auditorium taking the exam even to be considered for entry. I was never good at being tested academically, but I would become an expert at being tested by my life's experiences.

Nowadays, children are diagnosed with test-taking anxiety, ADHD, and who knows what else. Then special provisions are made for them based on those testing results. In the seventies, we didn't have those luxuries; you either passed or failed, you were diagnosed as being dumb, or smart!

When I started seeing people leaving because they had finished the exam, I began to get antsy. I wasn't going to be the last one sitting there! I started selecting my answers by doing *'eenie, meenie, minee, moe'*. My thoughts of joining the military ended that day. I wouldn't be serving my country, I'd continue spending my time serving Hakeem. I told myself I would excel at something (*and I did*).

I'm sure Hakeem had mixed feelings about how well and how quickly I learned the art of making love. He found himself being led, instead of being the leader. There were times when it seemed the only thing missing was a leash around his neck. He would be up under me, in my space all the time. I'm not complaining though; a dog is a (wo)man's best friend right? We became inseparable. Never a dull moment! We went to lots of concerts. The Whispers was our favorite group. Truly, he must've had stock in the hotels, as much money as he spent there. The friends we made as a couple even gave us a signature song "Always and Forever," the hit by "Heatwave."

Imagine us with a "signature song" -- the lyrics:

"Always and Forever, each moment with you. It's just like a dream to me that somehow came true. And I know tomorrow will still be the same. 'Cause we got a life of love that won't ever change..."

Or so I thought, until I ran into Hakeem in the supermarket with a lady and a couple of kids. You see, we had this chemistry, and somehow I just knew, when he glanced at me looking like a deer caught in headlights, something was not right! At that very moment, I realized *"we did not have a life of love,"* and from that point forward things would definitely change.

Honey was bitching about me finding a job! She kept saying I wasn't going to loaf around the house all day doing nothing! She had no idea what I was going through, and I did not want to hear anything she was saying! The only thing I wanted to hear right now was Hakeem's voice with an explanation of who that lady was with the kids? Part of me was upset with myself for not confronting him, but it was the little children that made me opt out of acting like a fool!

I ignored a rumor I'd heard in high school implying that Hakeem was an old married man because he gave me no signs of being married. He was ALWAYS around more than any young boyfriend I had in the past. Besides, by the time I'd heard the rumor, I was already hooked.

Hakeem had never mentioned having children, but I knew without the shadow of a doubt, that little girl whose hand he was holding was his! She looked just like him!

This was the era of no beepers, cell phones, or social media. I just had to twiddle my thumbs, pull my hair out, drink alcohol and wait for Hakeem to call. Days would pass before I'd hear anything from him and that was rare. I'm sure he needed lots of time to come up with a lie he hoped I'd believe.

Finally, Hakeem just showed up, ironically right after the delivery of two dozen lavender roses. He was dramatic, so when the tears began to flow before the lies, I wasn't moved. I just sat there, waiting in silence. Honey was not home to help bridge the awkwardness, and his mom had recently moved from the apartment upstairs. I could've made small talk, but I wasn't catering to him! I threw a roll of toilet tissue at him to dry up his fake ass tears then I asked, *"Who was the lady you were with?"* He responded, *"My wife, but we were separated!"*

*"**Really**? You didn't think I needed to know that you are a married man? How many children do you have?"*

He started to explain, *"I am not in love with her anymore, sometimes I ask myself was I ever? She's my friend; she's had my back since we were teenagers! I had five children, lost one; this took a real toll on our already tumultuous marriage."*

As my questioning continued, his mood changed, and he yelled, *"Wait a fuckin' minute!"* (men are experts at flipping it and making you feel like you did something wrong). *"I am not going to sit here and be interrogated by you! I love you! I think I've proven that. I came here not to go back 'n' forth about my wife, but to let you know I am moving in the vacant apartment upstairs."*

"What?? That apartment has four bedrooms? What are you going to do with all that space?"

"Well, not I, but we. My family needs me, and since the owner of this house and my mom are best buds, she has given me a really good deal on rent."

"Hakeem??? Have you lost your mind?"

"No! My wife is cool, you'll see."

As if we would be living like *"Sister Wives"*, this asshole said with confidence, *"Either you're going to accept it or not!"*

Not!!! *"Get the hell out of here!"* I started throwing the flowers at him, and since he was moving in slow motion, I picked up the glass vase and threw that too! He would call, pleading with me to understand, as he tried to convince me that he was still going to be by my side. We could still do all the things we were accustomed to doing. He even assured me she would not interfere. I didn't know how that was possible, but I wanted so much to believe him.

Three weeks later, I would hear men talking in the hallway. I peeked out of my window only to see a big U-Haul truck. The day I wasn't looking forward to, had finally come. The man I called mine, who really wasn't, would now be my neighbor.

It was mid-March. It was cold outside. I saw another shadow downstairs, but that person never came up. Curiosity would get the best of me, so I walked down to see who was sitting on the sun porch that was not insulated. It was her and that same little girl. I wanted to walk past them with an attitude, but I couldn't. Surely they were cold and had done nothing to me. I introduced myself, *"Hi, I am Kamara; I live on the second floor with my mom."* She responded, *"Very nice to meet you, I am Barbara this is my daughter. We are your new neighbors."*

As Hakeem and another man were lifting a sofa up the stairs, Hakeem smiled, that million-dollar smile, then paused and introduced me to his helper, *"This is my cousin Shahid, Shahid this is Kamara."* He never even looked at Barbara.

Shahid almost dropped the sofa looking at me. He then smiled and said, *"Nice to meet you, Mara."* I responded, **"Kamara!"** Who was he to be giving out nicknames and he just met me? I heard him laugh, then asked Hakeem, *"Does she have a man?"* He didn't respond.

A plumber was working on their toilet and the little girl had to pee. Reluctantly, I had to let them in. I couldn't let that child pee on herself! This began my relationship with my new neighbor who happened to be Hakeem's wife. ***What a mess!!***

I was learning there was a lot more to life than hanging out with Hakeem, especially since he was attached. We were still in a 'relationship' or whatever you want to call it but I was contemplating how to get out of it. It was getting ugly. Barbara would invite me up to their place once they were settled in. What would be my reason to refuse her invitation? I certainly couldn't tell her the truth! Unfortunately, I would meet all the little Hakeem look-a-likes running around. They were so innocent and cute, but I was too, when their daddy took away my innocence. Barbara seemed so sweet and kind certainly in time I would see another side of her. An answer to why her husband would rather have a teenager opposed to a grown ass woman. Getting to know her would only complicate things, therefore I was compelled not to do so. I would try hard to avoid her as much as I could. My heart had grown cold dealing with Hakeem and all of his shenanigans. I kept telling myself, I didn't give two cents about his wife! My loyalty was to him, right? She had even told Hakeem to ask *'the little skinny girl'* downstairs (*me*) to babysit sometimes. When he told me that I was pissed! I'll be her little skinny girl alright, and her husband's too. I started playing mind games with myself trying to focus on finding something to dislike about her. How dare she call me skinny, when I **was** probably about ninety pounds soak-n-wet! *Was that all I could come up with to dislike her for?* I had to find a way to ease the guilt I was beginning to feel from sleeping (well, not exactly sleeping) with her husband.

In the past, it was easy not being able to put faces on those crying children when their daddy did not come home. It was also easier not being able to put a face on the heart broken woman, when her husband didn't come home. Sometimes it would be for weeks because he was with me, making the motel owners richer. Things were so different now with them being my neighbors. Hakeem with his family living upstairs was without question, **not** the ideal situation. I could smell the inviting aroma coming from their kitchen. I could hear the pitter patter of the little feet running above my head. Surely, these were shoes I could never walk in. At this point I wasn't even interested in walking in them. I am still a teenager not of legal drinking age. Is there a legal age for being sexually manipulated? The walls were so thin I could hear the children screaming, *"Daddy"* with excitement as he walked in. The reality began to sink in for me. Hakeem, the man I loved, was not only someone's daddy, he was someone's husband too. No matter what he told me, no matter what I wanted to believe, his responsibility was to them and not me.

Every weekend this damn family had something going on -- a cookout, a baby shower, a birthday, a funeral, or something to party about above my head! Hakeem was so jealous, and he hated that I had the freedom to leave my house without his permission; he had to stay behind and pretend to be the faithful husband. He would soon find a way to fit me into the family plans. He told me his cousin had a crush on me. Then he commanded that I pretend to like his cousin (Shahid) too. How foolish of me to go along with all his deceptive schemes. Even though I was seeing Hakeem under a new light, I still loved him. These were times when both of us seemed obsessed with each other.

I could've won an Oscar at pretending to be Shahid's girl. The family was so happy to see him in a relationship. If I had asked him to jump, he would have said *how high;* if I had asked him to run, he would have said, *baby how far?* Now I was family too and according to Shahid, he was in love. I was reluctantly getting to know Barbara quite well, it was inevitable. She would tell me all kinds of stories about Hakeem, many of them were hard for me to believe, but I knew she was telling the truth -- *love ain't blind!* The more I got to know her, the worst I began to feel. I did not like what I had gotten myself into. It was time for me to move on. It wouldn't be easy but it would be the right thing to do. If there was any place lower than the gutter, Hakeem and I belonged there.

There were nights I would grab my blanket and sleep in the living room because I could not stand to hear what sounded like their headboard knocking against the wall along with the moaning and groaning. Of course, he kept his promise. I didn't go lacking either, many nights he would sneak in through my bedroom window. When Honey was sound asleep, I was able to do a little moaning and groaning too. I guess ole' Dr. Feelgood had two cakes and was eating both of them.

Chapter 4

❖

The Raging Bull

The relationship between Hakeem and me was heading nowhere. The only thing he was interested in was screwing me at his convenience and swelling my brain with lies. I was appalled the night he asked me to marry him in the backseat of his car. He told me that it was a custom for Muslims to have more than one wife. To this day, I don't know why I decided against it; I had gone along with everything else! If I'd believed in witchcraft, surely it would be confirmed that Hakeem had worked a root on me.

Now I was eighteen and I was transforming into a woman with her own mind, learning slowly but surely how to make her own decisions.

Life was moving right along; and so was the partying. My mother would finally be fed up with me entertaining all day in her house while she worked! The straw that broke the camel's back was the day she found out we drank all her liquor and put water in the bottles! That was it! I would have to find a job ***immediately***!!! Well, *immediately* never came, so Honey set up an interview at her job and told me when to be there and who to ask for.

In the seventies it wasn't what you knew, but who you knew that made the difference. I knew Honey and she knew the director of Human Resources. I was hired on the spot. This was the beginning of my healthcare career. I was loving my job, meeting new people and feeling confident. There were office parties for every occasion. I would also meet up with my co-workers for "Happy Hour" sometimes after work. Back in those days, we were never carded as long as I could pay for my liquor, I was old enough to drink.

You couldn't tell me I wasn't a full fledged grown woman. I was working two full-time jobs. The first one at Martland Medical Center and the second was working my body for Hakeem.

In the meantime, things with my neighbors got worse. Fear would smack me to my senses the day I thought my ceiling would cave in. I could hear Hakeem and Barbara arguing and the children crying. The rumbling sounded like an earthquake!

Suddenly, Barbara came dashing down the back stairway banging on my door as if her life depended on whether or not I opened it. There was no way Barbara deserved to be treated this way, especially when I knew all that was going on behind her back. What could have made Dr. Jekyll turn into Mr. Hyde? I had yet to find out. This situation was far too serious for me. I'd never been beaten as a child, and if this was some fetish of Hakeem's, I wanted no parts of this. Barbara's face resembled that of Joe Frazier's when he fought Ali. Her babies were with her -- their faces were streaked with tears and painted with fear. As far as I was concerned, Hakeem should've been more than satisfied with all she did as a wife! This was some crazy shit!

What was he thinking? Was he thinking? How could he beat her? How could he beat her in front of his children? Just who was this maniac I'd fallen in love with? Would I have my turn in the boxing ring too? Only time would tell...

Chapter 5

❖

The Perfect Gentlemen

Somehow in between the chaos, I was able to maintain my nine to five. Honey and I had been having some disagreements, so I asked my sister if I could live with her for a little while? Even though I never expected this living arrangement to last, I was thankful she said yes. You must understand, Kyndra hated Hakeem! She said, I was the only fool that would entertain his BS other than his wife! One rule she'd make crystal clear was that he wasn't welcomed in her house, ever!!! I was counting on her rules to help me get on with my life without him.

Rooming in with big sis was not so bad. I started seeing less and less of Hakeem. Anyway, what did he have to offer besides what I should have had enough of? Hakeem never really had a nine to five. He was, however, a full-time hustler, or should I say an entrepreneur in his own right. He was always well dressed in his designer suits, Rolex watches, gators and smelling like Creed Green Irish Tweed.

When he wasn't traveling by way of the friendly skies, he had a brand-new black and white Cadillac Coupe de Ville. Who wouldn't want to cut a deal with this businessman? He would travel from state to state, ripping businesses off by selling fake jewelry. But with his charm, no one would ever question whether it was real gold or diamonds. He knew just what to say and do. To top things off his sidekick, gopher, right hand man, Shahid was side by side taking orders and assisting Hakeem every step of the way. I had finally stopped playing the girlfriend role with Shahid. He was far too nice and his sister started figuring out what was really going on. When she confronted me with a butcher knife in her hand I didn't take her threats lightly. I took them seriously and promised to end the bullshit with her brother!

I had my eye on this handsome hunk at work. His name was Nick. Just to give you a little visual, he was a combination of Idris Elba and Denzel Washington. **Yessss...** fine as Elba, with deep dimples that you rarely saw. He wasn't a talker, so you know a smile was definitely far and few between. His walk -- so eloquent with those long bow legs.... *Denzel all the way, baby.* When I was standing on the ladder, supposedly filing – *please!* -- that was my ringside seat for watching his fine ass strut back and forth. So, I asked my co-worker what she knew about him? She would say everything negative as if nothing would work in my favor. First of all, he's from Guyana. Normally I would have turned up my nose, but after Hakeem, a little change in culture was probably just what I needed. That didn't discourage me; she continued saying that she was sure I was too skinny, and I was definitely not his type! It wasn't long before I realized she had her eye on him too. Therefore, time for me to make my own moves, do my own investigating. Sherlock Holmes had nothing on me.

He seemed very shy, introverted, totally the opposite of me. The gossip going around the office was that he was an arrogant, unfriendly asshole, but most importantly for me, he was single as in unmarried!

One day during our office downtime, I was showing off some new photos of myself when Nick came over to take a glimpse, I was in awe. He bent down and whispered in my ear, can I have one of your photos? *Mr. Introverted* was all up in my space, but I liked it. I hoped my co-worker was lookin', *bald-headed bitch!* If only people could read our minds. I'm so glad they can't. No time to play hard to get especially at that moment. All I could think of was Billy Dee Williams in "Lady Sings the Blues" when he was handing Diana Ross that money and, *No, I wasn't gonna let his arm fall off.* I gave him a photo so quick and autographed it with my phone number. The games Hakeem taught me how to play were now working for me! To my surprise, Nick didn't let any cobwebs grow on my number, he called immediately. He did not seem like the bad guy my co-workers painted him to be. In fact, Nick seemed to be the perfect gentleman.

As we began to secretly date, he'd open the car door for me and did sweet things like buckle my shoes or leave a love note on the console. He enjoyed taking me to New York to the movies or going on long drives just talking -- no touching -- as we got to know each other. This was a side of men I had not been introduced to. Unlike Hakeem, Nick had a real job, a nice sports car, and he was no senior citizen. He loved R&B and Reggae. We would listen to a lot of Temptations & Bob Marley. Oh, and I can't forget about Michael Jackson who was another of his favorites. It became very interesting rediscovering what it was like dating someone my own age again.

Unfortunately, there were too many times I'd find myself reminiscing about Hakeem and all of the adventures I had with him. Nick was laid back, a drama free type of guy. He appeared to have all the qualities of a good family man; however, there were no sparks in our relationship or should I say the explosions that I had become accustomed to. My evenings were now more like sitting by a campfire. *Hell, bring out the marshmallows and hot cocoa!* Instead of learning to enjoy the serenity, I had begun to feel like a damn nun! I'd gotten so programmed to my body being used by Hakeem that I didn't know how to appreciate Nick. In any girl's dreams, Nick came pretty close to having the whole package. You know, fulfilling every need until that rainy, cloudy day we decided to call out from work and make it happen. I was anxious, built up like it was my first time. Almost felt like it; it had been a very looooooong six months.

We did it, had sex, made love, whatever you want to call it. **"IT"** was too quick to be called anything!! I never uttered a word to Nick, but to myself, I had a lengthy conversation. My mature self decided that he deserved a second chance. Furthermore, I needed to grow up; *sex wasn't everything, was it?* It was extremely hard for me not being sexually satisfied, mainly because Hakeem would make it his business to pop in and out of my life. He would appear in places that normally he would never frequent. I swear someone in my circle was not my true friend. Someone had to be Hakeem's informant. He made a vow that he would **ALWAYS** be a part of my life, and he lived up to his word. I knew the time would come when I just couldn't resist him or the way he'd make me feel in bed.

Chapter 6

❖

This rollercoaster of a life I was living, filled with lies and deception, continued. However, just when I thought the real fun was about to kick in, the excitement suddenly started to diminish. This thrill ride seemed to be winding down, losing its excitement and the passengers on it as well.

Nick and I were no longer a secret and, of course, those nosey women at work were talking, especially the bald-headed one -- *remember her?* She was the one who said I was too skinny. I'm telling you, she wasn't the first one to throw that skinny word around! Bitches had better start checking history, cuz back in the 70s, skinny was definitely the new thick! We didn't know anything about no damn butt injections or no boob jobs then. That came a few decades later. If you didn't have any boobs, you just got some toilet tissue and stuffed it in your bra. Sergio Valenté or Jordache jeans were as close as I was gettin' to Gucci or Prada. Our dudes weren't askin' for all of that!! Now, those were the days when everything was entirely natural -- the real days, those "Soul Train" days when we didn't have computerized "filters" to create an image of who we wanted to be.

I wasn't spending my money on any of that stuff if we did have it because I was *'moving on up'* and saving for my new apartment - a luxury high rise located right in the heart of downtown Newark. The Hallmark House had an intercom system, valet parking and 24-hour security. Now I could entertain whoever I wanted, whenever I wanted to. I felt empowered until Hakeem found out and rained on my parade. It was like he and Nick were playing hide n' go seek, and my biggest fear was this game was not going to end with *a tap on the shoulder, you're it!!!*

Honey would allow me to dig my own ditches, but she was always there to catch me before I fell in. Many things would happen based on my lifestyle and Honey couldn't rescue me from everything, but she would surely try. Having my own place wasn't as much fun as I thought it would be. Sometimes it was lonely and scary. One night as I was enjoying the view from my ninth floor apartment picture window, I saw something that passed by very quickly. I had no idea what it was until shortly afterwards there were several flashing lights. I learned from the security officer that someone had committed suicide. I'm thankful I was too scary to look down. Rumor was, brain matter remained on the concrete. To be honest, I could've given up my lavish lifestyle then but I felt safe so I stayed.

Then, as usual, an unexpected wrench was thrown in the mix. I was forced to give up this fabulous new life and move back home. Who else but mom do you run to when you suddenly find out you're going to be a mom yourself? Many of my friends left home as teens, they couldn't go back and the majority of them didn't want to. I could go back to Honey wherever she was, even if she lived in a one-room shack; she would always have a place for me. I told one person that I thought I could confide in about my pregnancy and she betrayed my trust! Perhaps she was the informant I knew was somewhere lurking amongst us.

So here comes Hakeem, not the one I thought I knew and loved, but the same animal who battered his wife, the Raging Bull! The tables had turned, and now it was my turn to enter the boxing ring. I could almost see fire in his eyes! In my mind, I could hear my sister calling him *Satan*! Finally, I could see the striking resemblance. This was where real life began (or ended), filled with fear, challenges, and disappointments. The scariest part that I faced was that Honey would not be able to add any cushion to the bed of thorns on which I had landed.

"Pregnant!!!" Hakeem shouted, *"Who in the hell is the father?"* His interrogation hurt worse than the blows that would follow because I didn't have an answer! After all, for six months, the three of us played hide n' go seek, remember? Why would it matter to him anyway? The entire world knew Hakeem didn't need any more kids. He relied on his mommy and his wife to support the four he already had. His oldest child wasn't from his marriage. He wasn't even positive if the little girl was his daughter or his sister? Hakeem and his father, lookin' like 'Big Red' from 'The Five Heartbeats', were screwin' the same woman!! *Talking 'bout the apple not falling far from the tree!!* It was Hakeem that took the toddler because the mom had taken some bad drug and her mind ran off and never came back, just like Hakeem's dad.

How humiliating it was for me to have a knot on the back of my head from being bashed up against the wall and my eyes damn near swollen shut from crying. When Hakeem pulled up to Nick's mother's house, I stayed in the car. Nick came out, at this point, you would have thought Hakeem worked for law enforcement because he started interrogating Nick. Nick's answers were those he thought would protect me. I couldn't wait til' this nightmare ended.

I was so humiliated that in the middle of the interrogation, I opened the car door and took off running, as if my scary ass was really going somewhere in the dark, in the winter, in New-ark! When Hakeem pulled around the corner, he reached over, opened the door and yelled, *"Get your ass in the car!"* Without hesitating, I got right in. After that, there was silence the entire ride home. When I reached my destination, I got out and tried to slam his car door off the hinges, hoping the force would break the windows. I did not look back.

Nick and I would remain friends. Hakeem would vanish! Despite all the drama, my pregnancy was great. Having someone who proved they cared, regardless of the circumstances, was even greater. What a blessing to have a true friend and my mother to stand by me during what could have been a very difficult time. The two of them made it possible for me to create pleasant memories that would last a lifetime.

Chapter 7

❖

My First Diamond

Six months later, I delivered a beautiful baby girl, then post-partum blues... The baby had many of Hakeem's features, including his smile; she was beautiful. I was praying that she hadn't inherited his ugly ways. It was hard to enjoy what should have been one of the happiest moments in my life because I was concerned about Nick and what he must be going through. Damn! Hadn't he been through enough? I know he'd always hoped the baby would look like him. Nick continued to teach me by his actions what the qualities of a real man were. His love for me never changed; it may have even grown stronger once the baby arrived. As we stood looking through the glass at Clara Maas Hospital we didn't discuss who she looked like, we only discussed what a good life "our" beautiful little girl would have. Little did Nick know inside of my brain was a whirlwind! I was now responsible for another life. Perhaps I had not done so well with mine, but I intended to go the extra mile for her. She was my precious jewel, my Diamond, so that's what I named her.

Hakeem's informant obviously shared the news of my baby being born but I was a few steps ahead of her. Sometimes it's the person closest to you who is putting the dagger in your back! All the while smiling in your face but gathering information to exploit you at their first opportunity. How many of us know, our enemies can't do us any harm if we know where they're coming from, " *I knew.*" I had finally narrowed it down. Hakeem tried visiting the hospital, but I had already restricted all visitors. Once I was home from the hospital, the congratulatory calls didn't cease. One of the callers was Barbara, who excitedly wanted to stop by. I knew I couldn't hide forever, so I suggested that she and Hakeem come together. My phone would ring several times following my conversation with her, I stopped answering. DNA was non-existent back in those days, but in our world, a baby's parentage was determined by the meeting of the matriarchs; and as far as we were concerned, that was pretty darn accurate. If the mothers found a matching dimple, similar shaped foreheads, or the same shaped lips as the suspected father, that was confirmation enough. Even though I didn't need any confirmation, perhaps Honey did. Putting a seal on it didn't come with any monetary rewards. Who was I supposed to sue for child support, Hakeem's mom? Nevertheless, Honey's mind was made up. She bundled up my precious little jewel and off she went to show, with matriarchal determination, that this baby undoubtedly belonged to Hakeem. When she returned home several hours later, all she would say was that Diamond's grandmother (Hakeem's mom) thanked her for sharing this jewel. *Make a note* -- Hakeem and Barbara never stopped by, and my life was free from them for many years, but not forever. I can still hear my mom saying, *"The dirt will come out in the wash!"*

My life now was more like a carousel, moving in slow motion. Our only outings were to the movies, dinner and Dairy Queen. Nick was in love with Diamond and Honey was too. I was thankful for all their love and support; however, I was rather bored. I had sense enough to know this was the right life for my daughter but was this the right life for me?

Chapter 8

❖

𝔉𝔞𝔦𝔱𝔥

My friends were always talking about the good times they were having and begging me to come just once. I was pretending to be content, doing the same ole things every day and acting like some old ass married maid! I think part of what I was feeling was out of obligation; but hell, ain't no ring on my finger!!! One night I decided to take them up on their offer. It was most certainly a night to remember. It was the first of many nights filled with fun that became etched in my mind and still remains there today.

It was the early eighties, *Club Eleganza*, 16th Ave, Newark, New Jersey ("The Male Dance Review"). Didn't matter if it was a bitter cold wintry night or a sweltering hot summer night, we'd park blocks away and walk, sometimes even in our heels, to get there. We became obsessed with watching these handsome young men shake their almost naked asses around us screaming, out of control, intoxicated women!! I can remember one night there was a winter storm advisory warning, strongly suggesting that people stay at home! Honey was not happy with me hanging out every Tuesday night as if I was working a part-time job. She had the nerve to make threats! *"Stay home!" "Take your baby with you!" "Don't try me!"* Many times, I'd wish she had exercised her authority much earlier in my life instead of waiting until I was an adult and a mother. It's kind of hard adhering to discipline when you've never had to. I would always sit and listen to her lectures as she yelled like I was hearing impaired, knowing good and damn well once she fell asleep I'd be gone with the wind!

Let me give you a little insight on how much of a priority it was to be in attendance with my girls...

One night Faye (short for Faith) crashed right into a parked car! As she tried to back off, the car continued to slide all over the icy road. My heart beating a mile a minute! After that, I thought we would head home once she gained control of the car, but we just paused for a few, took a couple of deep breaths, and you already know... The party must go on -- and did it ever!!

Let me share a little with you about my girl Faye! We lived in the same neighborhood back in my Johnson Avenue days. I thought she was my age, but when she approached me, asking if I'd be interested in making a few dollars babysitting for her five kids, I dismissed that thought. With that many kids she couldn't be my age. I did run it by Honey, then decided to earn a few extra dollars. We lived in the same building, so I wouldn't have to be away from home, just a couple flights up. Faye was a widow. Her husband passed away long before we met. Every weekend I'd show up to watch the kids. The job was easy, but it was hard to believe that such a young woman held it down so well. The children were very well behaved, even the 1 year old. Her fridge was loaded with food, drinks, and snacks and there were no limits to what we could eat. The apartment - immaculate. There were times I'd sit mesmerized looking at the moving treasure chest in the colorful fish tank. Faye was a fashionista and was sometimes a neighborhood topic of discussion because nosy bitches couldn't figure out how she did what she did. She had so many wigs, shoes, and clothes that some nights I didn't even recognize her. She became my idol and my mentor. She was no young Black welfare recipient lurking around the mailbox on the first of the month for a check! She had a master's degree on being a go-getter. She worked three jobs to take care of her children if she needed to.

Time went on, and I got old enough to hang out too. I had grown tired of listening to her exciting stories when she returned after an evening of fun. It was like somebody turned on the lights in my brain! I'm single and don't have any kids, I wanna hang out too! As a team, Faye and I found my replacement to sit with the kids, and then we became an inseparable duo! Honey trusted her, which gave me more leeway, if that's possible. I would stay at her apartment for weeks sometimes, and even when I wasn't there, she was my alibi.

There was never a dull moment with Faye! She would always go from one extreme to another. She found out that one of her old boyfriends was incarcerated. She wanted to do something nice for him, so we were up half the night preparing a food package. The inmates didn't have to eat that high sodium bull shit out of the vending machines. They were privileged to eat home cooked meals.

Who let the Dogs out...?

So, for the first time ever, I was going to a prison for a visit. Faye invited me as if we were going to some gala event. It was a long and drawn-out process. She was comfortable; she had done this before, but it was very degrading for me. Female officers that damn near looked like males. They were rubbing my breast and in between my thighs!! Doors were clanging behind each corridor. I felt like the lion on the Wizard of Oz when, out of fear, he turned back and ran while heading to see the wizard! This place felt like a zoo, and I have never liked the zoo. As we passed all the security stops, we entered this big room with people everywhere. Some of the men looked like dogs in heat! I dare not make eye contact with anyone! We sat in these hard ass plastic chairs and waited.

After what felt like an eternity, but was probably only 15 minutes, two inmates came out. Faye whispered with excitement, *"There he is!! Girl, ain't he fine?"* Then she hit me with, *"The guy with him hasn't had a visit in God knows when. Will you just talk to him?"*

First of all, the friend was about 3 feet tall, and it was those platform shoes he was wearing that gave him **that** much height! We had a nice chat, and by the time the visit was over, I agreed that I would write to him. Faye would brief me on the types of letters I should write, and I became a pro!! I was getting more letters than I could respond to. You would've thought I was Mrs. Claus and it wasn't even Christmastime. I should've known something fishy was going on.

I would keep visiting him just to hang out with Faye. It seemed harmless until he told me he wanted a future with me, so he needed to be totally honest. *A future?* **Ah, hell naw!** Then he blurted out that he couldn't read!!! **What the...** So, who was reading my letters, and who was writing me back??? Finally, I started asking Faye to find out from her friend some answers to my questions. **Noooo...** All of these men were accused of some type of sexual offense and, of course, this dude I was visiting was *innocent* of raping a little boy and burying him alive!!! This bastard couldn't "READ" but he could "RAPE!" I reached **my** verdict that day -- *"Guilty as charged!"* When the guard's voice was amplified throughout the room, alerting visitors to get their final hugs so the dogs could return to their kennels, I knew this would be my last time visiting a prison!!! I vowed to myself that I'd NEVER return. *Remember to never say never...*

Faye apologized for not telling me that the men in this prison were all accused of committing a salacious crime. She didn't want me to form a negative opinion of her friend because she believed he was innocent. A year later, she would marry him and like two peas in a pod, I'd be right by her side supporting her decision. This would be just one of the many events that would take place for the duration of our friendship.

Chapter 9

❖

𝔐𝔢 𝔗𝔬𝔬

Thank God for Faye, always there, no secrets, no judge-
ments, my true "ride or die." I could share anything with
her. I remember sharing an experience about a wound I
thought would never heal. I call this my "Me Too" experience.

It began as a normal summer evening. I was at our hangout,
"The Peacock." Faye decided to stay at home. I felt comfortable being there without her because the owner was a friend of
Honey's. I'd been hanging in this bar since before I was of legal
drinking age. By the way, I was still not of legal drinking age --
that's twenty-one, right?

About a month prior to this night, Faye had gotten into a
scuffle with a woman who mistook her tiny frame for weakness.
This woman had been itching for a confrontation with Faye for
months. She would roll her eyes, pretend to accidently bump
into her -- just little kiddie shit! Faye would just ignore her. We
knew she was jealous because "Slick", a very popular guy she
liked, was always up in Faye's face and not hers. We would just
laugh at her!

Faye was a cute little chocolate drop, and hadn't done anything to entice "Slick", while this chick would go out of her way
to get his attention. She wore tight miniskirts, hugging her tail,
lookin' like it had dimples in it with all that cellulite. And those
big ole milk jug titties looked like hound dog ears! Her makeup

was so thick on her face she looked like a corpse. She wore this headband adorned with fake diamonds that came to a point in the middle of her forehead. *You get the picture right?*

There could be no ignoring her this night. Perhaps, she had too much to drink or was just showing off in front of her entourage. Later, she would wish she had minded her own damn business. She walked up behind Faye and said, *"Can I speak to you outside?"* Faye looked at me and said, *"It's time, let's go outside. I've had about enough of this Cleopatra lookin' bitch!"* Just before we walked out I saw Faye reach behind the counter and grab a bottle of liquor.

Immediately, 'Cleo' with all her friends egging her on, started talking shit, really loud. She called Faye a black ass, skinny bitch! Everything following that happened so fast. Faye cracked that bottle on the ground and then went straight for Cleo's face! Blood was everywhere! People started screaming, *"call an ambulance!"* while big bad 'Cleo' was down on the ground bleeding profusely.

Faye looked back and said, *"Next time watch who you're calling a bitch - **"Bitch"**!*

There were no cell phones then; we had time to get away before the police arrived. We ran to Faye's car laughing as we could hear the sirens coming from a distance.

Now, I am back at "The Peacock" but this time alone. I was there only a few minutes when I made the mistake of having to pee. When I walked into the restroom, there they were – five of them. I became the perfect target for revenge. I was immediately surrounded by all of them in this tight, one stall restroom. Suddenly, 'Cleo' became tough again, talking a lot of shit with that big scar upside her fair skinned forehead! When I saw that scar *(Faye's branding)*, I was laughing inside just like the night it happened. I ain't gonna lie though, that night I was scared; I knew I couldn't win. Hell, I was no Jackie Chan, and there was no room to move or run. I wasn't about to ruin the reputation Faye had already established for us; so, I talked just as much shit as she did, and reminded her that she was still a "Bitch", as I invited her outside with one hand in my pocket pretending to have a weapon. Did she really think I meant outside for them to possibly jump me? I was just trying to get outside of this restroom unscathed.

As we exited the restroom, the owner looked up and obviously sensed something was wrong. He signaled for me to sit down and he whispered something to 'Cleo' and her crew. He knew all of us. I felt relieved when he offered me a ride home and poured me another drink as I waited. I was then able to exhale.

As I sat drinking vodka and grapefruit juice I felt safe and protected. When he mentioned having to stop at his place before taking me across town I was okay with that. I can remember everything about this night as if hitting rewind in slow motion.

We entered an underground parking lot in a luxury building. It was clear by the cars that this was no cheap spot. He invited me up, but I said, *"No."* I didn't mind waiting in the car; afterall, he said, *"This was a quick stop!"* He wouldn't take no for an answer; he insisted that I come up. Perhaps, that should've been a red flag for me but, *naw*, he was Honey's friend. Surely, he has my best interest at hand.

Here I was, looking around, as he went into another room. It was really nice, so I didn't even realize he was taking so long. I was doing what I do, snooping around. There was a wedding album on the coffee table. I took a look, it was his wedding photos! Who even knew he was married, as many times as I'd seen him leaving my house. Oh well, it was none of my business that night; he my protector, or at least I thought he was.

Finally, he came out of the room – wearing only his underwear! I was in in shock! I never saw this coming. Suddenly, he pushed up on me, breath smelling like the bartender drank just as much as he poured for his customers! He licked my face just like a dog would do! Now I was feeling disgusted and nauseated! My eyes skimmed around the room looking for anything I could use as a weapon. There was nothing! not even a fork I could stab him with.

We were now having a shoving match, and he was becoming angry because I wouldn't let him stick his stinking tongue in my mouth! I am clinching my mouth tight and welling up some saliva to spit right in his face!!! Then I looked in his eyes. The man I thought was a family friend was unrecognizable! He looked crazed! He screamed at me, *"You know what you came here for!!"*

My thoughts: *Really, Mr. Huxtable, bring out the Quaaludes because I'm gonna need something to survive this violation!*

He managed to thrust me on the bed and yanked at my pants. Trust me, this was no cake walk for him! I was fighting and squirming like a worm in hot ashes! I tried to knee him in his nuts, but I missed! It started to get crazier! By now, I was trembling and afraid, yet I refused to give in. I broke away, my pants fell to my ankles, slowing me up. My hands are shaking like an addict going through withdrawals. I couldn't get the damn chain off of the door; I was screaming, ***"HELP!"*** Surely someone in this ritzy neighborhood could hear me; it was past midnight and very quiet. ***"Please call the POLICE"!***

Now I could feel the heat from his hot, stinking breath on my neck! There's no way for me to escape. I heard a click when he locked the door, then another click from the gun he was now holding to my head. I saw my life flash before me. I still couldn't stop panting and gasping for breath. He said, *"Shut the fuck up before I shut you up for life!"* I was trying to shut up, but I couldn't! My thoughts were, just fuck this psycho bastard and get it over with. When you are being so horribly violated, you find yourself just painfully helpless. I couldn't compete with bullets; I knew I wouldn't stand a chance. He pulled me back to the bed and there I lay with the gun in eyesight to remind me of what could happen if I didn't succumb. I now accepted that stinking tongue, the hand that was damn near choking me to death, and those wolf-like teeth gnawing at my vagina until it was bloody and swollen. After what felt like an eternity, he finally collapsed on top of me after several jerking motions, like he was having a convulsion. Was he done? I certainly hoped so.

He got up, still looking somewhat deranged with blood on his mouth he muttered some phrase, *"Boom, Cooch."* I have no idea what that means. Was he going to kill me now? He just casually handed me a washcloth and towel then pointed to the bathroom. I guess he decided to let me live or either to make sure I died clean.

At that moment I could barely walk. My vagina felt like balloons with too much helium! My eyes looked Asian, they were so swollen. At this point, even if I took him up on his offer to wash, I still would feel extremely dirty from the inside out for a very long time.

My thoughts in retrospect: I would rather have taken that ass whooping from 'Cleo' and her crew, maybe even a few stitches and a ride in an ambulance instead of trusting *Mr. Huxtable*, and getting that ride from the pit of Hell. A ride that would invade the spaces of my mind for a lifetime.

Believe it or not, I finally did get a ride home. He even walked around to assist me as I struggled to get out of his car. He handed me an envelope with a wad of money enclosed. No amount of money could pay me for the trauma my body or brain had been through that night. No money would make me keep quiet either!

The following day I would share all the gory details with Faye and a minimal amount with Honey. I wanted so much for him to pay for what he had done to me! That wouldn't happen, he wouldn't pay! I now understand firsthand why so many women play the hush game!

My day in court would never come. I was ridiculed, called every name except a child of God. Yet the violent, sexual predator would continue to hold his status in the community as an upstanding entrepreneur.

I would become known as the promiscuous teenager that encouraged his behavior. The supporting facts would be that I was hanging in a bar under age and drinking. It was said that I had presented fake identification (*which was a lie*), and that I went willingly in his car and then to his house. He swore that he NEVER knew my age, *another lie!*

As this story concluded and all went down in the book of life, I now certainly have a clearer understanding of why some victims don't speak up or why some even wait decades to share their stories; because I was a victim, now turned into a victor.

It happened to *"Me Too."*

Chapter 10

❖

𝔐𝔶 𝔕𝔦𝔡𝔢 𝔬𝔯 𝔇𝔦𝔢

My friendship with Faye, my Ride or Die, grew even tighter as our adventurous lives continued. A few years after Faye wedded her prison beau she would end the marriage. She gave it her all, but he lacked the ambition she had. Faye wasn't about to work "three" jobs while he struggled to find "one." She asked him to leave, then handed him a garbage bag filled with the few items she allowed him to take. As he began to walk towards the door, she offered him a ride in her brand new 1975 Ford Mustang. He declined.

Our friendship would withstand the storms of life. After he left there was many nights of soaked pillows but Faye realized what she considered a loss was really a gain. We took a break from men for a while and spent time doing what we enjoyed - singing.

We would reject company by ignoring the knocks at the door. We'd lower our voices, turn down the stereo, and hope the invader would take the hint and leave! We were not interested! More than likely, it was some freak we met at the club hoping to turn her apartment into an after-hour joint, but they wouldn't get in and we wouldn't go out!

If we decided we did not want to be bothered it would be in the best interest of whoever tried to invade our privacy not to force the visit. I vividly recall one time when a couple of fellas we used to hang out with forced a visit on us. They could sing too, this is how we became friends. However, they were broke and never brought anything to the table but their voices and greed. They were always hungry! The next time they showed up we would serve them well. Have you ever heard of Gaines burgers (dog food)? Well, while they ranted, raved and licked their fingers, complimenting us on how good that meatloaf was, little did they know they were consuming a small portion of ground beef mixed with a bigger portion of ground Gaines burgers - Bon appetite!

We had no desire for the nightlife anymore. We were having fun, just the two of us, reminiscing over our past mistakes, exchanging laughter where there were tears, replacing joy where there was sorrow, and in our ignorance, thinking that as long as we had each other, we would be able to rise above any of our circumstances.

Faye loved the voice of Linda Jones and she could sing just like her, if not better. Honey always told me I wasn't the singer in the family; it was Kyndra with the voice, which is why she went to Arts High School for her talent. One thing about me, I never allowed anyone else's opinions to determine what I could or could not do. Faye and I would make our neighborhood debut duet singing, "It's so Hard to say Goodbye to Yesterday." I can remember neighbors wanting to come in to hear us. Faye would often joke about me singing at her funeral if she died before me. That wasn't exactly my idea of humor. We were young though so who's thinking about dying? We had our whole lives ahead of us. Many good things would take place as we matured. Our friendship/sisterhood remained strong.

Faye would marry again, this time to a man twice her age. There would be no discussion about his looks. Faye had taken that off of her list of requirements. He would be the best thing that ever happened in her life (as far as men were concerned). Isn't it funny as you start to get older you become more attracted to the beauty within? I am not really sure how Faye and Sam hooked up, but looking back, I suppose fate had a hand or two in it. Sam kind of looked like a short version of Morgan Freeman -- predominantly gray hair, pigeon-toed and had a very distinguished voice.

Even though Faye had been married twice and always did things in a very glamorous style, she never had a wedding. This time, however, her hearts-desire would unfold like royalty. Other than the groom, I stood closest to the bride on her big day and my little Diamond, the flower girl, was the epitome of beauty. Faye glowed that day like never before. Finally, my friend, my sister, and my mentor had found happiness and was receiving the love she so deserved.

I anxiously awaited their return from their elegant honeymoon in Cancun. I couldn't wait to hear all the details. I knew there would be so much more in store for the happy couple. Faye was so excited about their future. There had been such a change in her. It was weird, I can't exactly put my fingers on it. Maybe it wasn't for me to figure out, perhaps it was spiritual (something neither of us was too familiar with at the time). Sam brought another flavor to their relationship. He was a God-fearing man. How many know that God doesn't make mistakes. They were churchgoers, and Faye soon found her spot there too. She began leading the choir with her angelic voice! Sam supported any decision Faye would make, not like any of the former puppies she had previously dealt with, but like a husband who adored his wife.

Faye began to experience some health problems. At no time did we think it was anything too serious. Many years prior, a doctor told her she needed a hysterectomy. She was young, so she decided against it. This time, the doctor strongly recommended that she be admitted into the hospital for a few days just for some extensive testing.

No matter how long I live, I will never forget the day Faye shared with me the results of her test. I also remember her being so calm when she said, *"I have Cancer, but I'm not claiming it." "I agreed to have surgery in the morning. I'll be fine"*, she whispered with confidence.

It's So Hard to Say Goodbye to Yesterday

I thought to myself, she **WILL** be fine, she has to be. Her entire life had changed in so many positive ways, surely this God that she spoke so highly of, would allow her to live. I really had no idea what He could do, I didn't even know who He was. Aside from what Faye told me, all I knew was that you pray to Him before you eat and at bedtime. She never pressured me about attending church. Our sisterhood stayed strong, even as we traveled on different paths. We loved each other, talked at least every other night, and **ALWAYS** gave each other the ut-most respect.

I was 7 months pregnant when my obstetrician told me to stop visiting Faye. She said it was causing me too much stress.

It was a sad day for me when Sam called to tell me it was too late; the cancer had spread. Maybe age was a major factor in how he handled himself, but Sam was the glue that held us all together. I'm forever grateful for having him in our lives for such a time as this. I'm telling you, Sam had stretched himself beyond elasticity. He continued to work his full-time job, cared for those five kids, and visited Faye daily. He even tried to soothe my aching heart with kind words and memories.

My girl Faye was never a quitter; she fought the good fight until *The Bitter End.* I learned so much from that lady. She lived up to her name. Her "FAITH" remained strong. She was courageous, caring, glamorous, smart, beautiful and even though she's no longer here with me in the physical, she will always be in my heart.

The day of her departure I was not there. I would feel guilty for a very long time. Sam and Faye's baby sister would reassure me I had done all I could do. She was ready to go; she left peacefully. She made mention of Jesus coming to get her (*and so He did*).

The funeral was as if she directed it herself in her good ole Faye elegance kind of way. The street procession was led by the Newark Police Department. There were so many cars you would've thought the President was in town. As we entered the church I began to feel weak. I thought I had prepared myself for this day. I know now preparation is not possible in saying farewell to someone you love.

The church was filled beyond its capacity just like her wedding day (not even a year prior). Many onlookers were peering through the doorway. It touched my heart as I watched each one of her male friends bow down to take one last look at her, gently touch her, and some would even kiss her. Their faces were covered with sadness, most of them had vowed never to step foot in a church, yet they were all here.

I would hold on to my promise, sometimes panting in between breaths. My face drenched in tears when her daughter nudged me and whispered, *"Please, you can do it."* Barely able to stand, and not knowing where I'd get my strength from, until many years later, I stood, and someone handed me the mic. I would render that duet we made so popular back in our hood, only this time, it would be a solo.

"Yes, I'll take with me the memories, to be my sunshine after the rain..."It's so Hard to say Goodbye to Yesterday."

Chapter 11

❖

𝕽𝖆𝖎𝖘𝖎𝖓𝖌 𝕹𝖎𝖈𝖐

After my wild life with Hakeem, being with Nick should've been a welcomed breath of fresh air. Afterall, who wouldn't want a caring, sweet guy like Nick? Leave it to me, I missed the wild run. It was in my blood! It gave me the adrenaline rush I was accustomed to getting. Nick just didn't have that edge to keep me on a natural high. However, it wasn't about just me anymore. I had to make my decisions based on the life I was now responsible for, my daughter. In my heart, I knew Nick was a good choice.

We were young, Nick and I were only a year apart, yet he was like an old man trapped in a young man's body. Living back at Honey's made our relationship more tolerable. He had a curfew, so I knew his visits wouldn't stop me from going to the Eleganza; at least I was guaranteed a hint of excitement there!

Nick and I had both been going through some changes; his mother had become frustrated with what he would not do around her house physically or financially. She had gotten to be a chronic complainer. If there is ever a book written on parenting, please make sure there's a chapter titled "Don't Wait Until Your Children Are Adults To Raise Them" clearly then it's too late.

Nick's mom eventually told him to "Get Out!" When he dragged his feet and didn't move quick enough, she did something to him that to this day he has not forgiven her for. She threw his very limited wardrobe out of the back window with the dogs and their shit (literally). Now he had nothing except what he was wearing. The workplace was made aware of Nick's unfortunate situation because he wore that same outfit as if it was a uniform for the next two weeks! Word around town was that Nick was sleeping in a condemned building a few doors down from his mom's house. The way he had begun to look and smell, he might as well had slept in the yard with the damn dogs! The handwriting was on the wall as to how strong of a man Nick was, yet I ignored every warning. It became quite evident, as my roller coaster of a life continued, I liked learning things the hard way.

I still cared about Nick, but I just wasn't sure how to approach the situation. Honey raised me to be a strong woman and to always stand up for myself, so if anyone would ever put me out of any place, I wouldn't be sleeping in no damn condemned building. I'd make it happen for me and the people I cared about, by any means necessary.

I felt obligated to help Nick pull himself back together. First, I started looking for places for him to live. Not like his girlfriend, but more like his mother. I was comfortable at Honey's with Diamond, and I'd already experienced being on my own, so I wasn't ready to be living with no man, especially one who nobody wanted to sit behind at work!

So, I found him a really nice room in a house in a peaceful neighborhood in Irvington. It felt good to help Nick get on his feet and feel better about himself; after all, he was there for me when I needed a true friend. How could I ever forget that? Of course, the chattering at work changed and he regained his sex symbol status. I just wanted to get back to my rendezvous at The Club Eleganza.

Nick and I had practically been through the mill together; therefore, I assumed he would always be sitting around twiddling his thumbs waiting until I decided he existed. I was so wrong!!! Now that Nick had a decent place, soap, water, new clothes that I financed, and that cat licked Camaro, the party **was on** with or without me!!! While I was being entertained by half-naked men in public at Club Eleganza, my man was naked entertaining in private with his new side chick!!

Most nights after the club closed I would just appear at Nick's, and that was usually ok. This particular night things were different. I knew he was at home because his shiny, cat licked vehicle lit up the street like a street light. I rang the doorbell and waited, I figured he was asleep. I saw the flickering of a light that's when I realized he probably wasn't home alone nor was he expecting me at 2 in the morning. I had a lot of nerve, but my insides began to boil!! Hell, if it weren't for me, his dirty, stinking ass would still be sleeping in the condemned building! He must've forgotten who he was dealing with. Would I be forced to show Nick that I learned more from Hakeem than just the art of making love?

I would commit one of the crimes that New Jersey was ranked highest for...that's right, I cranked up that cat licked Camaro like I paid the car note! I drove off and never gave a thought about what might happen next. I'm the one who got it back after it had been repossessed anyway!!!

What I knew for sure was that this would get his attention and hers too when sleeping beauty and Prince Charles got up the next morning. If where they planned to go in the morning wasn't walking distance they wouldn't be going! No IHOP (International House of Pancakes)for them unless they hopped their asses on public transportation!!!

The following day I pulled up at Nick's like I was an Uber driver. He walked over to the car and I rolled the window down as if to ask him his destination. I must point out that Nick loved me, but his first love was definitely that Camaro! The words that came out of his mouth were short but very far from sweet. There was no doubt that Nick was fuming, yet, as always he kept his composure. I had no idea what to expect next but what I did know was that I had enough experiences with the raging bull (Hakeem) in the past to know when it's quitting time. Furthermore, if Nick became violent there's no telling what or who he might destroy, it just might have been me. He was the quiet type, and you know what they say about them. I used my common sense, nicely got out of his car and handed him the keys that I had gotten made without his knowledge. Somehow, I knew not to ask for a ride home. My homegirl was waiting for me around the corner. She laughed so hard and raised her hand for a high five as if I had done something commendable by taking his car. My friends looked up to me, so I had to keep my image. I laughed with her, knowing good and damn well on the inside my heart was broken because it seemed like Nick was moving on. It had never really crossed my mind the pain I had caused him more times than I wanted to count.

I was sure that once I returned to work after stealing Nick's car, he would have cooled off and forgiven me as always. To my surprise, Nick had taken some time off from work which was really rare, he didn't tell me. *Oh no*, I thought, what's really going on here? My close friend, Cassie, whom I called Caz, told me she had driven past him earlier that day with some hoochie momma in his car! Caz could've kept that; inquiring minds didn't really want to know. I had to keep that poker face as if I didn't care, because Caz was the one who was waiting for me around the corner during the car theft episode.

It had really taken its toll on my heart that Nick was off work for two whole weeks and was no longer answering my phone calls. I left so many messages the damn answering machine probably was sick of recording my voice!

When Nick finally returned to work, I must say he was looking as handsome as ever. All them bitches at work were back to hee-hee, haw-hawing, in his face but a few months earlier they were talking about not sitting behind his dirty ass!! Now he wasn't speaking to me and was trying to avoid even looking my way. I had to be my own therapist, having private sessions with myself to keep my damn job!

There's no way he's forgotten me -- every time he opened his closet and sorted through his wardrobe I should've come back to his remembrance! Now did he think he was that smooth and could just end our relationship like that? This ain't gonna be no "Diary of a Mad Black Woman"; I ain't limping off like a hit dog and I sure ain't writing this shit down. I'm confronting him, and whoever else is involved in boosting his ego. Hell, I've invested too much in this relationship!

I had to get my 'Sherlock' on to find out what was really going on and with whom? I'd heard the woman who had shifted his attention was a fashion plate and a 'hood chick'; she made a living stealing clothes from Bambergers. I was really beginning to feel like an idiot. I had charged up my credit cards trying to accommodate Nick, and now this chick could just go in the store and take what she wanted and never had to concern herself with finance charges! Damn!

Curiosity would get the best of me. I had to see her for myself. I waited for hours one day outside of Nick's apartment until they came out. I was definitely not moved by what I saw. She was a fashionista with a banging body, but she had the face of Celie from "The Color Purple!" I'd also learned that she lived in the roughest projects in Newark! No wonder she made a living by stealing; she probably held up supermarkets to feed her son, but I decided she wasn't gonna steal Nick. So, let the fireworks begin!

Fate wouldn't allow us many confrontations; however, I do remember a time when Nick was seen leaving his place with her. I don't know how he spotted my little green Chevy Monza almost camouflaged behind this huge oak tree, but he did; needless to say, he left her like a thief in the night, only it was broad daylight. This was my time to introduce myself to her. Then again, who was I to Nick? She'd soon find out, and he would be reminded just in case he had forgotten. I was Hakeem's honor roll student. I learned and took mental notes of everything he taught me whether or not it was a personal experience or a subliminal one.

So, I pulled up on Celie; it was apparent that she needed a ride. I rolled down my window and spoke, introducing myself as Nick's fiancée'. I had this cubic zirconia tucked away in my glove compartment for moments like these. Clearly, I was not Nick's fiancée'. There was no diamond and no proposals! I began speaking to her in a very condescending way, especially after I realized that she didn't even know his real name! She kept calling him Jamaal! I was like, *who in the hell is that?* She was quite upset when she noticed his cat licked Camaro was no longer where he parked it around the corner (probably out of sight) to eliminate anymore surprise thefts! She said, he had a dentist appointment and they had planned to spend the day in Manhattan. ***Oh really?*** I thought***, not today Bitch!*** I told her to get in and we could meet him at the dentist to settle this misunderstanding. Furthermore, I wanted to meet this fake ass Jamaal character!!

Somehow, I could see the hurt in her already hurt features. We remained cordial -- that is until she spotted Jamaal a.k.a. Nick standing in the doorway at the dentist. She began pointing and screaming obscenities at me! I guess she thought old Jamaal was gonna rescue her, little did she know. I knew how she made her living. She had boasted earlier about all the things she had bought for him. He thought he was the shit, for sure, with his stolen clothes on! First of all, I let her know Jamaal is not his name. That's how much he cares about you! It got very ugly and she started saying things they were doing in bed as if I didn't know what he was capable of. I taught his ass what to do! I had to go for the jugular!! *Does he eat your pussy?* Her stupid ass says, *"He don't do that yet."* I said, well you do it every time you kiss him, you're eating mine!!! We were so heated neither of us noticed old Jamaal had slipped out of the back door and his Camaro was nowhere in sight. I got in my car and sped off. Hope Ms. Celie was familiar with the area because she was on her own! I learned much later she had finally gotten caught stealing and was doing some time in a gated community.

Nick and I both learned valuable lessons from those encounters with Ms. Celie. I stopped taking Nick for granted and he was finally trying to man-up with me. It wasn't easy for either of us. I had to stop wearing the pants in the relationship and put on the dresses while he was attempting to not be hard, but just have a firmer approach as a man. Some women need that, I did. If I wanted "Mister Softee", I could get him from the ice cream truck!!

I was now spending much less time, if any at all, at the male strip club and more time at Nick's. I decided that I was going to be the only one he stripped for from this point on.

Diamond and I had gotten comfortable at Nick's. We would sometimes camp out there for an entire week. I knew from the time he signed his lease that he had no intention of making us permanent residents. It was a small place, but until he asked me to go home, we were staying. I sure didn't want him to get to know how bachelors really lived – he just might start to like his freedom.

Unfortunately, it wasn't always the greatest atmosphere at Nick's because after hours we would have to be really quiet so that his nosey ass landlord wouldn't hear us walking around. She made it clear that she had rented to a single man, not a ready-made family! Lucky for me, Diamond never fit the description of a terrible two-year-old; she was more like a terrific two-year-old. She would sit for hours sucking her two fingers, never making a sound. On the other hand, it was I who needed to be put in a straight jacket, with a muzzle on, to keep quiet!

Honey was not pleased with how I had begun to treat her house – as if it was the neighborhood truck stop – with all the running in and out. She started nagging and asking if I had someplace else to go. It seemed as if she wanted me permanently gone. However, that was probably just a fleeting thought because I knew she would really miss her little Diamond. I believe she hoped her nagging tactics would make me stay home more, but it did just the opposite. I started whispering the thought in Nick's ear that it was time for us to get a place together. He had the nerve to be resistant to the idea. It seemed as if he had finally developed a sense of independence, and who was I to start talking about a family plan? I'm sure there were times when Nick wanted me to go home. I felt the vibe on several occasions, but until he was man enough to say it, I'd continue playing dumb!

The day would finally come when Nick decided to tell me he wasn't ready to do the shackin' up thing! Of course, that didn't digest well, and actually, not at all for me.

My name means *"a teacher by experience"*, and I have always lived up to my name. Had Nick not learned that I ruled, and by all of my experiences thus far, I was clearly his teacher?! What he didn't know was there was a turkey in the oven. I was just waiting for the right time to tell him. Now would be the right time – *"I'm pregnant!!"* For a moment there would be total silence. No champagne toast, not even a damn wine cooler! Nick felt no need to celebrate. In fact, he shocked me when he asked what I planned to do? Suddenly, I remembered all the mixed emotions that I felt when I became pregnant with Diamond. Surely, Nick also remembered; but this was not the same situation. How dare he ask me what I planned to do! Just where do men get the idea that they can even suggest that we abuse our bodies by vacuuming and flushing their seeds? He should have thought about the harvest while he was enjoying the planting.

Chapter 12

❖

History of a Harlot

As always, when things weren't going my way, or my heart was taking a beating, I knew where I could run to seek refuge. My Honey would never fail me. She would have her arms and door wide open at any given time and under any circumstances. I knew my Honey would risk her life for me. She wasn't verbally expressive about love, but I felt her love by her actions.

My mom's mother, on the other hand, was an entirely different human being. My relationship with her was always strained and distant. She was not one of my favorite people, and I walked on eggshells when in her presence. I was told that my grandmother, Halley Mae, was a hell-raiser in her day! It was said, she wouldn't hesitate to cut you too short to shit if she had to. She was not described as a woman with all talk and no action. People knew she was tough and what she couldn't take care of with her hands she always carried a good old Gillette (razor blade) as back up. My grandmother would threaten to slice the wives of the men she dated especially when they were bold enough to knock on her door asking for their husbands! Halley Mae's saying was "If you feel froggy then leap." Hopefully, the only thing that would be leaping would be their mates out of my grandmother's house. Those incidents were way before I was born, but her core must not have changed much because as far as I could see, that lady was still raising hell! I didn't like her, and she didn't like me, or perhaps she didn't like what stock I really came from!

I believed Honey had been shielding me and making sacrifices to protect me since the day I was born. No matter how hard she tried, she couldn't protect me from everything. Once, without her knowing, I overheard a conversation between her and Halley. My heartless grandmother was threatening to tell my daddy why I resembled no one in his family! Suddenly and painfully that was a revelation of why my sister and I were nothing alike. I had none of the features of those people I thought I belonged to. Their genes were strong and they were all, without question, related to each other – except me. When my mother returned to the room, I closed my eyes tight and pretended I was asleep. I could never reveal to her what I had overheard. I held on to that secret all of my life until now. I carried so much guilt as most children do. I was guilty that Honey couldn't live her life because she was always trying to protect me. Guilty, because all I had to do was sniffle and my daddy would damn near lay roses at my feet for fear of losing Honey. If she thought for a second anyone was mistreating me they'd become history, my daddy included. I even felt guilty knowing that my sister was really his only biological child and he catered more to me. Such a heavy load to carry from a young age. These feelings would spill over into my adulthood, always trying to fix everything for everybody when in reality I was broken myself. Who was going to help me fix me?

Unfortunately, Honey would overcompensate as a result of this secret she was living with, and she would spare the rod when it came to me. She probably allowed one too many liberties where I was concerned. At about age fifteen I was propped up on a bar stool drinking Kioffa and orange juice; surely this was a time I should've been reprimanded. Many would say, had I been their child my lips would've been plastered around that straw for life! The decision of course, was not their call, they were not my mother! As life continued, I had a much clearer understanding of why Honey was so protective and lenient. I think she did a helluva job considering the role models she had in her life.

I don't know if it was a coincidence that I happened to overhear the conversation between Honey and Halley or if my grandmother purposely told my mother that day hoping I had my ear to the wall. The next thing I'd hear Halley say about me to Honey was "She's just like that man" and by her tone that wasn't a compliment.

My thoughts would forever linger. Who was this mystery man? Would I ever know?

Perhaps I was mimicking behaviors that I subconsciously learned from those women closest to me or maybe the similarities of the mystery man-- like when I continued my relationship with Hakeem who was married.

Talk about generational curses! I can honestly say Halley Mae passed down some shit!!!

It was a tradition that we visited Halley Mae who lived in Boston, Massachusetts every year! In spite of all the abusive history, I learned from Honey. It was evident that she still loved the old hag. It was absolutely no fun at Halley's! I hated it, I think Kyndra did too, but she would never say anything. Kyndra was her first granddaughter, and she was also Halley's favorite. Halley would spend quality time sitting at her baby grand piano singing gospel songs and praising Kyndra about how well she could sing. I can still hear the lyrics "Swing low, sweet chariot, coming for to carry me home." I just stood in the shadows wondering when they were coming, and could they move any faster...

Somebody, somewhere please carry this hateful lady away so I would NEVER have to visit this place again!

Mealtime at Halley's just added to the torture for me. It undoubtedly was no Red Lobster although many times there was fish on the menu. Honey had warned us, but she didn't want to hurt her mom's feelings. So, when Halley said, "I'll cook tonight," Honey just said, "Okay."

If there was ever anything I drank that may have tasted like toilet water, it had to be Halley's lemonade. She couldn't even make that! Her meatloaf had to be a dish from Hell! It consisted of anything leftover in the fridge mixed in with the ground beef -- fish heads, vegetables, rice -- *need I go on?* Her meatloaf was *shit loaf!*

Oh, and I can't forget about her two pets. There was Mewmew, a dusty gray cat that looked more like an oversized rat. His weight would increase while we were there because we generously shared Halley's cuisine. Of course, he was the only one who enjoyed mealtime at her place. Then there was that crazy, always barking dog. He was her precious Chow-wow pup. In his previous life before life with Halley, I think he was a Chihuahua, but somehow he lost his identity. Those animals loved her. So apparently, Halley had a few good qualities.

When Honey would go out to explore the nightlife, sometimes Halley would allow us to sit on her bed that was three mattresses high. We would learn about each of her treasured evening gowns with the most intricate details and each event she wore them to as if she was royalty. There was always someone's prince interlocked to her arm, but I dare not ask who. I'd just stay in a child's place as she would suggest when my big mouth would begin to ask questions. She would pull out dozens of photo albums and scrapbooks and tell stories that only a grandmother could tell.

Although my grandmother's stories were unlike those of my friends what they did have in common was that Good Lord they spoke of and the required perfect attendance for church on Sundays. So, what I understood as a child was that it was acceptable to the good Lord to raise hell all week, but on Sundays as long as you were a faithful churchgoer, there was a place for you inside the pearly gates.

The one thing that Halley did that left a good memory for us was our Sundays with her. Every Sunday she would rise before the rooster crowed singing loud and preparing for church. It was like Easter every Sunday because we had the opportunity to get dressed up with our bonnets, lacey dresses, ruffled socks, patent leather shoes and dainty white gloves accented with artificial pearls.

The cathedral we attended was beautiful but what I remember most is that I was tired of all that reading and was so hungry by the time they passed out what looked like crushed up crackers and a doll size cup of juice. I couldn't wait til' I got mine. I looked up to ask Halley why did they break up my cracker? She put her hand over my mouth, and I'm still waiting for an answer. What felt like six hours later, church was dismissed, and we returned to Halley's with our stomachs growling from hunger pangs. What awaited us would be our grandmother's soul food, food that would definitely claim your soul if someone wasn't praying for you...

Chapter 13

❖

The Silent Cries of the Innocent

Throughout the years a wall had been built between my grandmother and me. It was extremely hard for me to forgive her for all the cruel things she did or allowed to happen to my mom and her siblings.

My uncle, Honey's youngest brother, was someone I never had the opportunity to know. Unfortunately, he spent most of his life behind bars. He probably felt safer there. Honey once told me a story of how he was hit by a car on his way home from school.

He was so afraid of getting beat by Halley for taking the forbidden shortcut that he got up, bleeding profusely from his head, in an attempt to make it home. Luckily the driver who hit him followed him until he collapsed. I was sitting in awe as my mother told the story. It was hard to believe that someone, a boy no less, could be that scared of his mother. It's no wonder prison was sort of an escape for Uncle Lester. He had been pretty much a juvenile delinquent when finally, he committed the crime that would send him to Sing Sing at the age of eighteen. Honey, with tears welling up in her eyes, continued to tell of that fateful day that changed her little brother's life forever.

Uncle Lester and his friends robbed the neighborhood grocery store. How could they be so heartless when Mr. Troy, the owner, and his generosity, were the reasons many of them had food on their tables? Honey said, "The pot they were smoking caused them not to think" They were not even disguised, and Mr. Troy was able to identify my uncle but not the others. My uncle was loyal to his friends, he refused to snitch and took the rap for all of them.

Twenty-two years my Uncle Lester spent in prison. It was an oversight that he was not released decades sooner. When the discovery was made, there was no choice other than to release him that same day. It was like he had been evicted from his home. He had no idea how to fend for himself in mainstream society. He was now institutionalized and somewhat comfortable with how he had learned to live. He had not been reformed but had conformed to his way of life behind those walls.

My Uncle Lester was a stranger to me, a little brother to my mom, an idol to many of the inmates who grew to love him, and a derelict to the streets of Poughkeepsie, New York, where he spent his final days. Rumor had it that he froze to death in a subway station. Halley Mae would sugar coat things when asked what happen to her baby boy by saying he died of heart failure. Oh, Halley, the fuckin' harlot, lived in a big place where she was able to house exchange students but didn't make room for her own son.

In this case, justice would've prevailed by leaving my uncle behind bars. The pain of even being in the vicinity of Halley Mae was worse than the idea of incarceration.

My mom was the third of four children born to Halley Mae and Granddaddy Pete. She was the most vocal about all the drama that was going on around this 'special' family while her other siblings would pretend the horror stories never took place. They would leave their tormented spirits locked tight within to haunt themselves all the days of their lives. I had heard some older people say Halley Mae must've made a pact with the devil, whatever that meant.

Me, like my mom, would absorb all that she had told me and when the time came for me to visit with my cousins, I'd have their undivided attention narrating the biography of our parents. I swore them to secrecy because I'm sure I wasn't supposed to tell them. Three of my cousins were boys growing up in Newark, New Jersey, having the reputation of being tough guys but there were times I even saw a tear stream from their eyes about the abuse their mom, my Aunt Peaches had survived.

It was after their parents divorced when things got really ugly! Variety seemed to be the spice of life for Halley until she decided to marry a preacher named Walt. Halley seemed to place men over her daughter's, something my Honey would never do! Another lesson I learned well.

Let the truth be known Halley was jealous of Aunt Peaches! She was gorgeous and glamorous. Long before weaves Aunt Peaches used to wear something called a fall. Kind of like half wigs or lace fronts (nothing new under the sun). She wore heels, makeup, driving gloves, always classy never left the house unkempt. To us, my Aunt Peaches was royalty.

Honey told me, Walt used to sexually abuse Aunt Peaches. It was another horrible story as they all were. She said, he would come in their room late at night. Honey was the little sickly child referred to as the ugly duckling. Aunt Peaches would always protect her, therefore, many times they would be sleeping together. That still didn't deter this bastard from fondling my aunt and more. So what if her little ugly sister lying next to her was sniffling. No one was sticking her anywhere! What the hell was she crying for? Of course, he threatened to kill Halley if they had told! You know what I'm thinking many years later! They should've told on that mean bitch!! Killing her would've deserved a reward. However, I'm just the daughter feeling angry for all my mom had been subjected to. The truth is abused children seem to love the hardest and Halley was still their mom.

Aunt Peaches had been accused many times of enticing the men Halley entertained, most of them belonging to someone else, of course. My aunt would then be beaten! It was almost as if Halley was trying to disfigure her pretty face by the ugly bruises and scars. On the outside, over time the scars would fade but It was the scars on the inside that did the most damage! A pattern followed Halley Mae's children; they were always searching for escapism. Perhaps each of them lived their lives in fear, the fear that someone would see inside of them and discover their deep, dark secrets.

Honey must've been at a point of no return when she (without telling her sister) decided to put an end to this man violating them. It was her turn to protect her big sister who always had her back. Remember, Halley liked old Gillette and now Honey would use what she had learned from her mother! It was dark, she said, and she was afraid, already crying but silently. While she waited for her prey she was not going to let fear overtake her, she never would, she never did!!! Finally, the moment she was waiting for would come. Walt, wreaking of alcohol, hands under the covers, same old routine but with a big surprise this time!!! As he began to slide Aunt Peaches panties to the side, Honey began to slide that damn razor blade right across his disgusting ass hands!! Blood was spurting everywhere!! Honey was panting for breath!!! She went berserk!! My poor mother, my poor aunt, my poor uncles too. Some women just should not have children! It was said that Honey had a nervous breakdown and was never,

ever the same again! She ran out of the house that night not looking, just running!!! Someone captured that ten-year-old girl with a nightgown saturated with blood. I'm thankful she was rescued and hospitalized and cared for. Granddaddy Pete would get wind of all this happening to his children, and he took them to live with him. Unfortunately, the damage had already been done. Honey never finished telling me what happened to Walt, it was far too emotional. He probably left Halley and moved on to another household with more little girls to violate. She had to take her medication and lay down. Perhaps, Honey should've never had children either, but she had us, and we loved her as she loved Halley. The rest is history...

Aunt Peaches jumped out of the frying pan right into the fire when she married an older, prominent businessman. Uncle Felix lookin' like Mighty Joe Young! He was well established, had a big house in Newark, NJ, and plenty of money which could even make Mighty Joe Young kind of cute. Honey would say, after I became an adult, *"Put a suit on a gorilla and a woman will fight you over him!"* And so you have it, let the fights begin for Aunt Peaches

Chapter 14

❖

The Fall of the Family

Kyndra and I used to love spending time at Aunt Peaches' house. It was exciting and different from what we were used to. Our cousins taught us how to play "Cops n Robbers" and "Bonnie n Clyde" games we had never heard of. They had toy guns, handcuffs and all kinds of stuff we had never seen. Honey was so protective; she was reluctant to even allow a water gun in our house.

I loved my cousins and most of the time we had loads of fun at their house. However, there were a few things that made me uneasy. Sometimes my cousin wanted to pretend to be my husband; I wasn't so fond of that. I would never tell Honey because I knew she would never allow us to go back. There was something about his behavior that just didn't feel right. Something else I didn't understand was why Aunt Peaches had no authority in her own house. It seemed as if in this house their grandma ruled! Aunt Peaches couldn't give permission for anything! Her children bypassed her and waited on their grandmother's approval.

Aunt Peaches' life was far from the life she deserved. As the years seemed to roll by, Uncle Felix turned out not to be her knight in shining armor but more like the gorilla in a suit. She took verbal abuse from his ugly ass mother and was treated like the maid and Uncle Felix's personal secretary. After her last child was born, there was yet another change that darkened her life more. Under the pretext of giving Aunt Peaches some extra help in the house also giving her more time to spend with her only daughter, Uncle Felix hired someone with questionable responsibilities. Aunt Peaches was so beautiful, on the order of the actress Diahann Carroll, but the newly hired help was more like Halle Berry. Right off the bat, the secretarial duties, for which she was hired, were blurred by her apparent personal relationship with Uncle Felix. She no longer referred to my uncle by his name, but instead called him "Feeley." How ironic, old Uncle "Feeley" was probably feeling more than he should've been -- right in the house with his family, how disgusting! If this lady had a car she would never drive it, Uncle Feeley was her personal chauffeur. When he would leave to take her home, many times he would not return unless it was after we were asleep.

This outrageous behavior went on for years! However, just like Aunt Peaches did as a girl by taking the physical beatings, now she endured the beatings to her heart until she couldn't take anymore. Thank goodness she found the strength within to divorce him. This took courage. Aunt Peaches had all the glam and glitz that a trophy wife could ever hope for, but once again, just like her relationship with Halley Mae, she was not getting the love she was so deserving of.

My cousins were older now and so much more aware of things, especially those things that were happening right in their household. They always bought my sister and me up to speed on life in general. They made us pay attention and we did just that. Their goal was to make sure their naive girl cousins from Poughkeepsie, New York became fluent with the city life and all the city drama.

It was so sad watching this family disintegrate, my cousins didn't adjust well to the fall of their family. Donnell, my cousin that was the closest to my age, my 'play play' husband that I never revealed to anyone. He committed suicide three years after the divorce. He seemed lost once Aunt Peaches left them behind. I can remember getting the news like it was yesterday. I can still feel the pain. I must fight not to let my tears drop even now, forty years later. I was at a friend's house when Honey called for me to come home. That was odd; she never did that, so I knew something was terribly wrong! When I got home, Kyndra met me at the door with a blank look in her eyes. *"Donnie is gone,"* she said. *Gone where?* I asked then she sadly responded, *"Uncle Felix found him in his room. He hung himself."* All I could do was cry, cry and cry some more.

Uncle Felix, with all his money, was so cheap! He actually was shopping around for a reasonable funeral home to bury his youngest son. I heard him say Whigham's Funeral Home was too pricey. He finally settled for some funeral home in north Newark. I don't remember the name of it, anyway, it no longer exist. As I walked up the deteriorating steps that sad day, I could see cobwebs wrapped around the stair rails. The wood floors creaked, and it felt so eerie as the gentleman escorted us into a small room off to the side. How would all of us fit in there? This was certainly an indication that you get what you pay for. As hard as it was being in this awful looking place, it was even harder as I took the short walk to look into the coffin where my cousin's body lay cold. His fingernails were dirty, and he needed the same haircut he needed the last time I saw him. If I could've seen his feet he probably had on the same dirty socks he was wearing the day my mom told him to take his shoes off at the door. She sure regretted having said that! The bottom of his shoes appeared cleaner than his socks. That was just a few weeks before his death. If only I had known that was the last time I'd see him alive, I would've given him the hug he looked like he needed. I would've thanked him for all the fun times we had as kids. I would've cheered him on one more time about what a star basketball player he was. I would've tried harder to help him find Aunt Peaches who had left him behind thinking her sons would be better off with their dad; but it was over, no more time to do anything. He was only seventeen.

Aunt Peaches looked like the pillar of strength as she stood staring at her baby boy's body. She again was consoling all of us as we cried in pain. Their grandma would scream, *"Please don't leave me Donnie"!* Uncle Felix passed out.

I later would see one tear trickle down Aunt Peaches' cheek, but that was all. She never made a sound. Donnie's life was over way too soon.

If Aunt Peaches had not endured enough pain, not too long after Donnie died her oldest son would depart this life also at a young age. JD was known for being a pimp and a womanizer. When he finally found the woman of his dreams and had a child, he became very ill. Everybody was really secretive about what was going on with him. His body just continued to deteriorate. He was quarantined in his own house. They kept his daughter away from him and he was only able to eat and drink from disposable utensils. They had fixed up a corner in the basement of the house where the dog lived for JD. Him and the dog became roommates. Whenever someone came to visit him, they had to suit up like they were getting ready to perform surgery. There was a time when Kyndra (who had become very religious) made his favorite - macaroni and cheese. When she went to deliver it to him she suited up and prayed from a distance. When all the macaroni and cheese had been eaten, he returned her corning ware. She accepted it with a smile but I later saw the dish in the trash barrel outside. It made me feel so sad. I used to sit and talk with him for hours, but I wouldn't suit up. There were times when he shared some deep secrets with me. He even spoke of karma being a bitch! When he cried, I wasn't afraid to hug him, and when his tears landed on my face, I didn't race to the bathroom for the facial scrub. I'm sure there were times when he felt so alone. My hopes were that God forgave JD for his past and gave him peace before his final departure. When he finally passed on, I'd hoped he was welcomed by a God unlike the one Halley served. I was not in favor of her God who obviously approved of "Raising Hell"!

In my opinion, Kyndra too had mimicked our grandmother's hypocritical behavior the very day she prayed for JD from afar, as if the disease he had contracted would somehow leap into her body! Not to mention the corning ware she trashed, insinuating dishwashing liquid and Clorox would not eliminate any of his germs. I thought, *why pray? And who would need this God they served anyway?*

Aunt Peaches still remained strong through it all. You would think she would've turned a deaf ear on her mom when she became bedridden and crippled, but she didn't. Halley became this frail old lady just sitting in her rocking chair waiting to be fed. Yep, my thoughts: *She would still be sitting there right now, as a skeleton.* Those two little girls that were damn near tortured as kids (now adults), just faithfully took shifts to ensure Halley had everything she needed until she took her final breath.

Honey would not attend her funeral, but my sister and I did -- not as loving grandchildren (at least not me), but to represent my mom. The sun was shining on me through the stained-glass windows of the church and that shiny coffin glistened. This was my time to sing as I remembered those times I was left in the shadows. I sang "Swing low, sweet chariot...and they came and hopefully carried my grandmother home.

Chapter 15

Ophelia

After years of lessons from three generations of strong, sometimes confused, and often stubborn and unrelenting women, I knew I could make a decision (good or bad) about moving on with my life at this point.

It's never good to walk away from a situation angry even if you don't get what you want, exactly when you want it. It took a more strategic plan to get Nick to see things my way (about us living together). However, I knew it was time to leave Honey's. How was that going to look - me, Diamond and a belly full waddling back home to momma. I had never officially left but I had been staying at Nick's for weeks. Even though I felt like I was standing in the middle of the Sahara Desert, I would not let anyone see me sweat. I too was as strong as the woman who raised me, I knew I could get through this period of transition too.

The good news was that my best friend from Clinton Place Junior High School had moved back to town! Ophelia, who I call "O", had been gone for years but we never lost contact. She never went into detail the reason for her return and I didn't ask. I was just ecstatic my best friend was back!

She had a son as a teenager which forced her to grow up a lot quicker than I did. Adongo was the name of "O's" son. She wanted to name him Maxwell, but Ms. Joann threatened to throw her out if she didn't name him what she had chosen. I thought, *what kind of a name was that?* I never told "O", but I had to say *"A Donkey "* to myself before calling him to make sure I pronounced it correctly.

She met and married a well-known entrepreneur who had a very established and thriving trucking company. "Dee Birds" was famous for transporting all types of goods from places all over the world. Herman was no small timer though because he was drafted into the NBA while in college but was injured early on in his career causing him to pursue other business options. Of course, he had many connections with his former teammates and his company soared! He was older than "O" and had no problems providing for her and her son. They seemed like a match made in Heaven. I was happy and sad when he moved her off to the sunshine state, sad because she was leaving but happy because if anyone deserved some happiness, it had to be "O."

Our upbringing was entirely different! "O" got the beatings that everyone thought my fresh ass needed. If things back then were like things are now, "O" could've called protective services on her mom and sent her on up to that 'gated community'. ***That lady was crazy!!!***

I used to feel so bad for "O." I always wanted to protect her, but the only thing I could do as a teenager was supply the Kleenex and listen. One night, Ms. Joann was hysterical because she came home from the bar at three in the morning and her newborn ("O's" baby sister) needed her diaper changed. Who would know that? It's three in the morning, and everyone was asleep including the baby. Ms. Joann was just looking for shit! "O" was awakened by that spike heel being yanked from her head, blood gushing!!! Get up bitch and change that baby's diaper before she gets a damn diaper rash!!! "O" reminded me of my Aunt Peaches, always protecting everyone and losing herself. As she continued telling me the story she said, her mom acted like the blood gushing from her head was sweat on a hot summer day...hurry up Bitch, then go wash your face!!! "O" never flinched, she followed the instructions of the slave master, and she followed them quickly or else. I often wondered was Ms. Joann jealous of her own daughter, like Halley was of Aunt Peaches.

"O" was so pretty on the order of Gabrielle Union with a figure like 'JayLo'. Her mom was shaped like a quarterback and looked more like Whoopi! "O" was never taken to the ER for that assault and she still wears the scars today both on the outside and inside too. There were too many stories to tell, and I tried to erase many of them from my mind. As "O's" younger sister grew up she would buck on Ms. Joann, and I must say, she had to be as crazy as her mom to do that!! One night she was tied to a chair, for bucking, stripped of her clothing and then whipped just like a slave!! Her body was bloody and covered with welts! Ms. Joann became angrier since her little slave wouldn't cry, she just clenched her teeth and bared it! Finally, after hours of abuse, Ms. Joann filled the tub with ice and told the bitch *(which seemed to be what she named her daughter's)* sit in that tub until the burning stops!! Ms. Joann was worse than my grandmother, and that's pretty damn bad!!

If I didn't know "O" so well I may have thought she married Herman to escape from her crazy ass mother, but she loved him. You couldn't tell her he wasn't Denzel Washington's identical twin. Clearly, she wore glasses and wasn't wearing them the day they met.

"O" and I decided to share an apartment for a short time until both of us knew which direction our lives would take. It was clear her and Herman were not together. "O" was not a talker and perhaps the reason for her return was too painful to talk about. We made an agreement that we would give each other time if we decided to get back with our men. Of course, that was my stipulation because I was still working on a plan. I was trying to get to where "O" had already been - married. My intentions were not to be running around with two kids and no man! That was not the path I was planning to take.

I'm telling you our sisterhood was so needed at this time! When you meet someone special, and your souls connect it doesn't have to be a male, female connection, it can be of the same sex, and somehow, you'll know that bond is forever. These are the relationships worth holding on to, not necessarily needing to talk every day but knowing when you need them, they'll be right there come hell or high water! That was us!

While "O" and I were learning to embrace the process that didn't stop things from happening. Adongo was not adjusting well to the absence of his stepdaddy. He was acting out in school! He was always an energetic little guy or like the old folks say, he was all boy, one that definitely needed a man around. "O" had become frustrated with all the parent/teacher conferences.

It was a tough decision to make, but It had to be done. "O" allowed Adongo's biological dad to come get him and take him to Hotlanta. She needed a break, and he needed a man so why not his dad?

These men always talking about, they got it, they can handle it, yet he dropped Adongo right off at his mom's place. She was beyond thrilled to have her grandson, so it all worked out. She had an ample amount of experience and help. She was the mother of five son's and three daughter's.

"O" and I laughed, cried went down memory lane and was thankful to continue traveling life's highway as new lanes were being created.

While I only knew about their lavish lifestyle in the big beautiful house in Hialeah, Florida surrounded by sunshine, palm trees, antique cars a Rolls Royce and their BMW's in the driveway. As far as I knew they were living the life of Jay and Bey. There was so much more that I was learning about what was going on behind the scenes.

You must understand Ophelia was never that type of person to live her life in the limelight. She preferred to live a quiet life with probably just one friend (me), driving a station wagon, drawing and hanging out with the children but instead she had to become the trophy wife Herman needed hanging on his arm with all the glitter, glam and dinner parties with the athletes and their wives. While my thoughts were, I'll take that life hers was you can have it with all the bullshit that comes along with it!

Back in the day before Adongo or Herman, when we were girls, we were known for our voices. We would sing in talent shows and in all the chorus productions! We would meet in the restrooms to practice making sure our harmony was pitch perfect. Our peers would often come up to us asking us to sing. Music is good for the soul, and it was good for us, our friendship, our bond. I'm sure it helped "O" create some happy times and forget about all the turmoil at home. One song that we would sing repeatedly was "Step into My World by Magic Touch" during those magical moments it was indeed our world, or at least we felt like it was.

So you can surely imagine just how excited I was when my BFF (Best Friend Forever) returned to New Jersey!

When we finally had an opportunity to get in each other's business "O" told me her return was not by choice. As a matter of fact, she loved Florida. However, it was Herman's decision suggesting a little space would do them some good. Space! Yeah right – space for him to lay up without the old ball n' chain! In my mind, I was giving her the side eye, but I kept my comments to myself, and this time I would learn to be a good listener, thankful she couldn't read my mind! The worst part of the story so far was she was in her first trimester of a difficult pregnancy with triplets! "O" already had two sons, Adongo and Jaylen (*so glad Ms. Joann had nothing to do with her youngest son's name*). I was so disappointed in Herman who, for many years, seemed like the perfect husband. Remember, I was on the outside looking in, but everything is not always as it appears.

So here we are two best friends reunited. As bad as our circumstances were there couldn't have been a better time for our reunion. Clearly, we needed each other.

I was too busy complaining and comparing my life to hers. Sharing my stories of hard work and still living from paycheck to paycheck sometimes having to hide my car in Cassie's garage to avoid repossession. I was blinded by the bling in "O's" life until she took the blinders off and reiterated what I already knew; everything that glitters ain't gold & everything that sparkles is definitely not diamonds! On the flip side, was a family dealing with more serious issues than I could imagine.

"O" told me their marriage began to shift when she decided she was no longer willing to be controlled. In the past she remained quiet and didn't speak up to him about anything; but the last straw was when she accidently grabbed his BMW keys instead of hers to make a quick run to the store. Even though this was not her first time finding shit that confirmed Herman's infidelity, this was the straw that broke the camel's back! "O" wasn't snooping. She was not that type of woman. As a matter of fact, she would have preferred not to know.

When the car came to a screeching halt on that rainy morning, the lipstick that rolled from under the passenger's seat caused "O" to snoop just like I would've done. She found a lot more than she bargained for. She pulled over and parked hoping to gain her composure and get her heart to stop racing. The only thing that was missing from under that seat was the Caucasian or extremely fair skinned woman that these items belonged to. There was a dainty Louis Vuitton bag that was obviously not closed tightly. The torrential rain was still falling like the tears from "O's" eyes as she continued to find lace panties size 2, a make-up compact containing a shade almost as light as pancake batter, receipts from hotel stays, florists, you name it....

Now it was all was making sense --the knock-down, drag out fights they were having, his complaints of her weight gain, as if going from a size 2 to a size 6 qualified her for an episode on the series "My 600 Pound Life"! After all these findings, she was just done, her brain was now in a fog. She returned home without the items she went to get from the store. As a matter of fact, she'd forgotten why she left.

She was no longer quiet and there was no stone left unturned. Herman, for once, would not even deny any of the accusations she made, and he made no effort to man up. He yelled obscenities, making everything that was destroying their marriage **her** fault! It was **her** weight!, **her** laziness!, **her** lack of wanting to attend all the social events!

"O" was not just sitting there this time, collecting his darts to destroy her; she was firing back! *"What about you Herman,"* she said; *"****your**** weekend excursions, ****your**** excessive drug use, and now alcohol too!*' Herman seemed to suck all that up, but when "O" screamed, *"Not to mention our making love; it has turned into just sex, and that shit ain't even good!"* *"I get more pleasure sucking on a damn popsicle!"*

As if he misinterpreted what she said, as men so often do, he stood up -- all 6 feet 5 inches of him, over her mere 5 feet stature -- with fire in his eyes, saying, *"So you are fucking someone else! Someone else does it better than me?!"* "O" said she didn't remember anything after that. She awakened in the hospital ER with her jaw bruised and wired. Herman was sitting at her bedside, rubbing her hand like the damn caring husband! Not sure of what he told the medical staff or how she arrived there, he whispered that he was sorry. She didn't respond because she couldn't.

Ophelia had learned some lessons from Ms. Joann; she was fragile, but she wouldn't break under pressure! I was proud of her. Her heart may have been broken, but her spirit remained whole.

When "O" recovered , Herman suggested space, no matter how devastated she was she welcomed it.

As time grew near for the babies to be born, Cassie and I got together on how we would help "O" through such a difficult time. Don't forget, I was still carrying a load of my own, but it seemed like nothing compared to what "O" was going through. Herman was like a ghost during this time. It was said he spent the majority of his time touring, visiting places like Italy and Dubai. Surely, he wasn't traveling the world alone. That just wasn't his style.

Herman came from a great family. His parents and siblings were there for "O" in any way she needed them. There were many times "O" ignored their phone calls, forcing them to just show up with groceries, gifts and sometimes money. Herman's mom was embarrassed at how he treated his family, but he was her first born and spoiled rotten, so she just tried to pick up where he left off.

The time would come for "O" to deliver those babies. I

would be the designee to reach out to Herman. That wasn't an easy task I would first have to call around to find out if he was in the states. You must understand this was before cell phones.

I wasn't successful at locating Herman, but I guess somebody was. I was there with "O" the entire time. Her labor got a little intense and she had to have a cesarean. Now she had 5 sons! Adongo, Jaylen, Aiden, Joshua and Jeremiah. I could see the look of fear in her eyes not knowing if she was capable of raising 5 kings as a single parent. We often talked about the possibilities of her and Herman getting back together. People always say they stay because of the children, but truthfully, she loved him. I knew it just like his cocky ass knew it too. Therefore, when he finally got around to visiting her I knew my place, I left, and had already prepared to leave the apartment whenever the time would come.

My hope was that he would humble himself and pledge his love for her and his son's! When I returned to see her the next day my hope was not fulfilled. "O" was not herself, she had been somewhat sedated. As she began trying to tell me what was going on, it was clear she had been given anti-depressants. Herman had asked her to give the boys up for adoption.

For a brief time "O" was pretty doped up on prescription drugs. That seemed to be the only way she could face reality. She had to be monitored on the psych unit before they would send her home with a newborn. Fortunately, Joshua and Jeremiah had to remain in the NICU (nursery intensive care unit). They weren't sick but needed to get their weight up. This would give "O" a little more time to adjust once she was discharged.

"O" later mentioned that she thought he brought divorce papers with him because he had an envelope in his hand. However, after the doctor pulled him to the side to elaborate on her mental state and how serious this was, Herman would glance back at her as he exited the room with a look she couldn't describe. It could have been anger, disappointment or even disgust? Whatever the look, "O" knew it wasn't the look of a man having any feelings of empathy!

Herman had only visited one more time after that and he still came with a bad attitude! He continued to pressure her about considering his suggestion for adoption; as a bonus he threw in he also wanted a divorce! That man never ceased to amaze me. He spoke as if he was offering some great two for one special.

When "O" first came home it was rough on her emotionally. She wanted to lay around and mope. Caz and I would not allow her to get comfortable in a slump. She had tried suicide once before, we would not let that happen again (not on our watch). It took awhile for her to adjust to the medications but once she did life started moving in the right direction. We convinced her to go to group therapy sessions and that ended up being the best decision ever! She was getting out of the house, meeting people who truly understood what she was going through. She would attend the sessions twice a week. I noticed she was fixing herself up now before going out. I was happy to see her taking pride in herself again. I should have known something was going on...

"O" had started dating a guy she met at her group therapy. When she felt comfortable enough to bring him home, it turned out he wasn't a stranger to me. I knew him very well. He was 100 percent Newark bred, Clinton Avenue hood. He now belonged to Temple number 23. As a kid he was Connor to us, but as a man he was now Rasul, another Muslim, hopefully **not** like Hakeem. As far as looks, he was totally opposite of Herman, so perhaps Rasul may have been just what the therapist ordered!

If you liked Hispanic lookin', El DeBarge Black dudes, then

Rasul is your pick of the day. In our era it was like a fad. You had to date at least one light skin boy with curly or what people considered *'good hair'* to be considered cool. I'd met my cool standards too, but that would be short lived. I was attracted to tall, dark men with big lips and facial hair. If you didn't meet that criteria, trust me, I wasn't serious. Otherwise, you had to have a personality that was out of this world! By the way, Rasul did have that quality. He had wit, charm, humor, and he was able to put the sparkle back in "O's" eyes, something I hadn't seen in a very long time.

"O" and Rasul seemed to be having the time of their lives. To this day I'm not sure how but Herman got wind of it. Perhaps Jaylen leaked it. Whatever the case it really didn't matter. "O" was finally learning how to move on. Herman kept his distance, so "O" figured he was content with his life as it was. Herman made it crystal clear he wasn't happy with "O's" decision to keep the boys, but there was nothing he could do about it except add more money to that child support. There was a hit song back in the 70's "It's Cheaper to Keep Her." For Herman that should've been a National Anthem! Even though Adongo had gone to stay with his biological family, Herman was still responsible for him too because he legally adopted him when he married "O." How ironic is that; he adopted a son but wanted his own son's given up for adoption. I just couldn't understand this kind of thinking at all. Perhaps over time Herman didn't understand either, but he did understand that it was definitely "cheaper to keep her." If the truth was known, it was eating him alive knowing that "O" was moving on and was at a happy place, even with five sons on her back! She was carrying her load as if it was weightless, no longer depending on him, but displaying the strength that she had buried by allowing him to control her.

Don't you tell me what a woman can't do or what a woman won't do! We are the most powerful when adversity strikes!

Time waits for no one, wounds heal but sometimes scars remain. After much needed therapy, not from just Herman and his shenanigans but from a childhood filled with mental and physical abuse from Ms. Joann's psycho ass, Ophelia had finally begun the healing process. It was very noticeable in a positive way. Not only did "O" get her hour glass figure back, but also her self-esteem.

She would always look so well put together when she went out to her support group meetings. No one would ever know by looking at her what an uphill battle her life was. I would care for the children while she would go out. Diamond and Jaylen were a big help with the babies. They were growing up slowly, but surely.

Herman would do very rare pop ins and mostly when "O" was at her meetings. He would occasionally take Jaylen to a car show. He would make small talk with me. Most times, he would just stare at the dynamic three, which is what I called the babies, with that look that we just couldn't pin point. There were also those times he would go in "O's" room. I hated that because to me he was violating her privacy, and since she had recently started dating, I wasn't sure what he might find. However, I knew my lane when it came to Herman and "O", and I stayed in it. After all, on paper they were husband and wife. It was never a secret whenever Herman stopped by because the scent of that big cigar hanging out of his mouth lingered.

We started seeing a lot more of Herman. He seemed to be *cock blocking,* as they say. The more we saw Herman, the less we'd see Rasul. It wasn't hard to see what was happening. He was interacting more with the babies and Jaylen was in his glory. His daddy was his hero. There was even talk about Adongo coming back home. All the signs were there, Herman was reclaiming his territory. I too, was being watchful always using my peripheral vision for the things going on in my own family. All the signs were there for me too. Nick and I were at a good place. My strategy had worked and now would be the perfect time for us to find a place of our own. More than likely this would also be the perfect time for Herman to join his clothes that were building up little by little in Jaylen's closet.

Nick and I were in touch consistently. He would occasionally take me and Diamond out to Dairy Queen and to the movies. I think he was getting bored with his bachelor pad. Nick wasn't the same type of man as Herman. I know he missed us. My learning to stay calm and remain quiet was working. – that was out of character for me.

There would be a change of hearts for both Nick and Herman, and hopefully we would all be able to live happily ever after...

Chapter 16

— ❖ —

No More Free Milk

Nick and I decided to move into the apartment complex where Honey lived on Prospect Street. It was a nice quiet area located in East Orange, New Jersey (a suburb of Newark). I would soon have two children and was not ashamed to admit that I needed and wanted to be nearer to my mother. When we are young we seem to be in a hurry to get away from our parents, yet when we become older and somewhat wiser, we want to be closer.

Nick and I would never see eye to eye on the subject of parents. He didn't give a damn about his mother, and rumor had it that his father may have been a tourist who was visiting Guyana at the time of his conception. Whoever he was would always be a mystery. It was quite evident that Nick held grudges because he had not spoken to his mom since she threw his clothes out to the dogs years ago.

I've heard that as women we need to pay close attention to how men treat their mothers; it somehow symbolizes how they may one day treat you. I wasn't sure if this was a superstition or fact. In due time I would find out.

Nick had changed a little during our time apart. Even though he was still sweet and introverted he was a lot more confident with a voice. I liked that! Nothing would change his love for me. He would jump through hoops if he needed to and I would need him to jump quite a bit.

So, it was 11pm and I was 9 months pregnant! I have a taste for Kentucky Fried Chicken! Time to jump! Nick had dozed off listening to a smooth Marvin Gaye track. I nudged him, he got right up, I got up too. He said, he'd get what I wanted and bring it back. You're probably thinking, *awww how sweet* , and you're right but not for a pregnant woman who wants hot chicken wings with mashed potatoes n gravy. I'm going too.

Here we sit in the drive through because the queen doesn't feel like waddling inside, she just wants what she wants! There are probably about three cars behind us when I looked at Nick to tell him I thought my water just broke! I hadn't felt any real bad contractions, but maybe I wouldn't since this was baby number two. Neither of us knew what to expect because with Diamond, my water never broke. Poor Nick had to get out and start directing all the midnight chicken lovers to back up, so we could go to the hospital. Needless to say, I didn't get my hot chicken wings that night, but I got something far better!

Our son was born two hours later at Orange Memorial Hospital! Everything happened so quick but not as smooth as we had hoped for.

Perhaps you know the routine in the labor and delivery room, if not, just to brief you -- a few select people are in the room -- nurse, doctor, your preferred coach, in my case it was Nick. There were a few hard pushes, lots of excruciating pain, beeps from monitors, deep breaths and usually at the end of all that, a baby crying!

Our baby came out, we heard nothing but a voice over the intercom calling for the NICU team (a team called when something is wrong with the newborn). Our son's skin color was lavender, and he wasn't breathing! My heart racing, Nick's lips were white, his dark face even began to look pale as the team of people hovered around our son. ***"What's wrong!"***, I yelled, then I heard my baby finally let out a yell as they whisked him away like a flash of lightning. I'd never seen Nick move so fast, but he was right on their heels, never looking back. Did anyone even remember I was in the room? My legs still in stirrups, bright lights shining, all I could hear was the tick in that giant clock staring at me; it was now 3:23 in the morning...*where's my baby?*

Nick finally returned with the doctor. His lips were no longer white, his dark skin was no longer pale, which let me know our son was at least alive. The doctor explained - the umbilical cord was wrapped around his neck; the more he pushed the tighter the cord got. It was choking him. That is why he was discolored as he was losing oxygen, and for a quick second we had lost him.

Nick and I were beyond grateful for the medical team that morning. They were absolutely great! During the pregnancy we talked about naming our baby after Nick, but due to his rare entrance into this world, and his strong nature to survive we agreed to name him Gem. Gems are extremely rare and absolutely great; they are a precious stone. Now our family was complete, we had our Diamond and our Gem.

Nick loved having a son. He was so attentive to him. Sometimes he seemed obsessed. When we did our grocery shopping he would put more matchbox cars in the cart than food. Nick was very artistic. He would make these little cities out of sneaker boxes. Whenever we had company they were amazed at the cardboard cities Nick created. I wondered if this was really for Gem or was Nick living the childhood he missed growing up in poverty? Nick would tell me heartfelt stories of having no shoes but still having to walk to school in the sweltering heat. The scars on his feet would always be a constant reminder of what his childhood must have been like. It made me always thankful for what I had as a child, and now what we were able to provide for our children. However, as time went on, I would have to put Nick on alert. There were two children in the house, not just one! How about a bracelet, a doll, a coloring book, or something along with those matchbook cars that kept creeping in to the house? By the time Gem would really appreciate them, there would be hundreds!

I didn't want to make a mountain out of a molehill, as Honey would say, however, I was going to keep looking with a side eye. I knew Nick could never forget that once upon a time there was a man named Hakeem -- his genes were in full effect in our little Diamond. I'm not saying Nick was showing favoritism; it may have been simply because Gem was a boy; but just in case, I hoped he knew Kamara was **ALWAYS** watching and no man would ever take precedence over my children!

Honey was not a meddling neighbor, she minded her business. She liked Nick and felt like they had something in common because their birthdays were only a day apart.

I was taken aback when Honey asked how long I intended to shack-up with Nick? She threw in her little philosophy saying, *"Why should a man buy the cow when he can get the milk for free?"* I had been giving free milk here and there, and she never said anything before. I guess she didn't like me playing house as her next door neighbor. Honey gave me this long lecture, something I wasn't used to, especially coming from her.

She told me men didn't marry women who gave them what they needed without a commitment. I would never be blatantly disrespectful to my mom, so I wouldn't say what I was thinking.

My thoughts -- Many times*, not always*, children mimic what they see. No offense to Honey, but she was married once, now divorced with four daughters, and three, maybe four different fathers. So, who was the committed one in our household, and now how could she teach me about commitment?

Regardless of my feelings, Honey's advice wouldn't go away. Perhaps, she didn't want me to travel down the same road as she did. I glanced at my body and Honey's *farmer talk* started making sense. My body was starting to look like a cow -- that may not be too easy to sell.

Sorry Nick, no more free milk...

I'm sure you've heard the phrase *"You can lead a horse to the water, but you can't make him drink."* **WRONG**! I led the horse (*the horse being Nick*) to the water and made him drink it too!

Not too long after Honey's lecture this cow was sold to the horse!

Our wedding was on a budget - *my budget*, yet it was still beautiful. Ophelia and Herman, back in love again, were very much a part of the ceremony. "O's" hands were really gifted with the sewing machine; she made my dress perfectly -- had me looking like Versace designed it just for me. Nick would let me have my way with the wedding plans. All he needed to know was where the ceremony would take place and what time he needed to be there. This was a clear sign not to do it, but no time for analyzing. We were getting married. That was final! Herman would be the Best Man and "O", the Matron of Honor. Diamond was our beautiful Flower Girl and Jaylen, our handsome Ring Bearer. Our wedding party was just simple and sweet.

Nick started speaking to his mom a few months before our wedding would take place. I thought that was the right thing for him to do before we started our union. I found out later it was only a part of his plan to persuade her to buy my wedding band. This was another sign not to do it, had I known this before saying "I Do."

Something old, something new, something borrowed, something blue and something RED is what I would have on my wedding day. Once Nick bought the cow, he wasn't getting any milk!

We recited those vows *in sickness and in health, for richer or for poorer until death do us part."* The melody from the song that was sang *"You and I can conquer the world."*.. would probably hold more validity than those vows we repeated.

Face it, I already had two children, bad credit, and a wedding band purchased by my mother-in-law. The man that was promising to take care of me for the rest of my life couldn't afford the wedding band I wanted. **Nevertheless...** On a cold, but sunny winter afternoon in Newark, New Jersey, Nick and I became one. I don't think either of us realized what we had committed to.

The handwriting was on the wall. We should have never been married, but we'd ignored all of the signs.

After the ceremony, things would be right back to our normal life. Nick and Diamond went to pick up Gem from the babysitter and I hopped in the car with "O" so we could laugh and talk about the wedding and those Dollar General gifts. I was more interested in what was in the envelopes. We needed a box spring and mattress. I was tired of sleeping on that thin ass futon!

Oh well, no sense in crying over spilled milk, free milk, who bought the cow, or who made the horse drink the water! We were family now, so we might as well give it our best shot at making this a holy matrimony and not a *hellified* one.

Nick and I grew so much closer as husband and wife. I'm not sure why, perhaps it gave both of us a sense of security. We had been through so much, so young. I guess our love proved to stand the test of time.

As a family we did everything together, the four of us were inseparable. Of course, there were times when we wanted to go on dates (just the two of us) but that didn't happen very often. It's fair to say Honey was still sowing her wild oats, living the life she felt she lost having children as a teenager. In addition to that her biological clock was still ticking, and I had two, much younger sisters. Honey was having a hard time being a mom during this second phase of her life; so, being a grandmom was certainly not on her list of 'to dos'. Nick's mom would have loved her role as a grandmom, but she wasn't the ideal housekeeper, and this limited her time spent with our children. I couldn't imagine our children having to use the bucket in her room opposed to the toilet in the cellar. The conditions were deplorable. This big white bucket sat next to her bed as if it was a nightstand. The odor was horrible, just imagine (if you can) a plug in scented with week old urine and human shit!

Nick shared stories with me how it embarrassed him during his youth whenever he would have a guest that needed to use the bathroom. Most of the time he would lie by saying someone was using it. I unfortunately got to witness the bucket first-hand. It was one of our very few dates as a married couple that Nick's mom welcomed having her grands over. She accused me of being bougie and not wanting my children out of my sight. Being over protective was a trait I inherited from Honey, but that had nothing to do with me being bougie. There was not a bougie bone in my body.

Once I'd seen that damn bucket she could call me anything her dear heart desired, but our children were never going back over there unless they were glued to my lap and if they had to use the bathroom they were going outside in the bushes!

Marriage would definitely be a learning experience for me and Nick. Hopefully, we would survive by trial and error. We had no role models to mimic in the happily ever after. We were truly on our own in this venture.

Nick was a loner, most of the time he was content spending time with me and the kids. I, on the other hand enjoyed having my friend's around. I knew as a married woman my place was at home, therefore as a compromise I started having get togethers for any and every occasion. I was never a sports fan but when it was time for the " Superbowl" that was a great time for a party! I'd have one. I wasn't a sales person either but Tupperware, Avon, Amway, MaryKay let's have a party! Christmas, New Year, Thanksgiving, Halloween party at our house! My friend's already knew bring a bottle or a dish and let the good times roll! Nick was forced to mingle!

On one occasion, I remember getting an eerie feeling that something was wrong. Caz had not arrived and she was the queen of parties. It was not like her not to show up. Her boyfriend Pat got on my nerves but I always welcomed him because she loved him. He had to be the last of the "Superfly" era with his slicked back S-curl and his long cashmere coat with the fur collar. Both Caz and Pat could dress. We would spend the first ten minutes after their arrival discussing their attire. That's probably the only thing these two had in common.

The following day I would learn that my intuition was right. Something did happen much worse than I imagined. Caz was in the hospital fighting for her life! The CBS news had reported a near fatal accident on South Clinton Street. The picture of the car that flashed across the screen was so mangled there was no way to identify the make or model. I had no idea it belonged to Caz until her sister called me with the news. I raced to the hospital immediately!

It was so sad to see my friend laying there appearing lifeless with tubes everywhere and fragments of glass glistening in her hair. Her leg was in a cast propped up and her face was bandaged mummy style. The good thing was the machines were still beeping and the life line was in clear view. She was still alive! No one knew the details of the accident except her and Pat, ironically he was nowhere to be found!

When Caz regained consciousness she was in a lot of pain. She began telling us bits and pieces of what she remembered. I began to dislike Pat's trifling ass even more.

They were headed to my house but had already been drinking. Pat's driver's license was revoked for non payment of child support. Imagine that, this deadbeat walking around in the finest fashions like he's ready for a photo shoot with GQ magazine but ain't paying for the well being of his damn children! Then always got his unlicensed ass behind the steering wheel of Cassie's brand new vehicles!

Caz remembered the impact when out of nowhere the car slammed into a fire hydrant! It erupted from the ground, the water forcefully spewing as if waiting for the neighborhood kids to come cool off. She wasn't wearing a seatbelt, it wasn't required. Her head hit the windshield so hard it shattered! She felt Pat pulling her painful nearly lifeless body across the seat to position her as close to the steering wheel as he could. Shortly after that, she heard sirens and passed out. It was clear Pat was only thinking of himself. While Caz sustained many life threatening injuries Pat would walk away unharmed.

Months later while Caz was still making a slow recovery, Pat would show up! His first question would be if she planned to share the insurance settlement with him! I'm not sure of her response but as far as I was concerned he belonged right with her car in the junkyard!

Chapter 17

❖

No Winners in this Game

Our family would continue to grow when I became pregnant with our third child. Going through the motions and emotions of childbearing was old news, and it didn't seem like a very big deal for either of us. Nick catered to me less this time around. He was more concerned about the high cost of childcare, and if we would ever be able to spend any quality time together alone.

We had developed a little system just to give ourselves an outlet. Nick spent his individual time at the gym to stay in shape, and my time was spent eating out with my friends, getting more out of shape.

Herman would get wind of our little arrangement and started inviting Nick to hang out with him and his former NBA buddies to shoot some hoops, as they called it. Nick would tell me Herman was giving him advice on how to spice up our marriage. I know Herman didn't expect Nick to come home and tell me, but he did, and I was heated! Perhaps Nick's sudden interest in wanting us to date, when I was damn near nine months pregnant, was probably his way of trying not to follow Herman's advice. Those of us who knew Herman knew that his idea of spicing up any relationship was by cheating! I don't know what was going on in Nick's mind during this time, dating (in or outside our marriage) just wasn't going to happen. The one date that we would keep would be on a hot summer night in June when our second son decided to make his entrance into the world in less than 30 minutes after our arrival to the hospital.

There was something extraordinary about this little boy right from the start. Unlike his siblings, he came out screaming, letting everyone know he was very much alive. Maybe that was a sign of what was to come. I'd read somewhere about the onyx crystal, a powerful warrior stone known for stomping out negative thought patterns stemming from debilitating and toxic emotions grown out of fear. The name Onyx seemed fitting for our little warrior, and so it would be. Welcome to our world, as complex as it had started to become.

Everyday was the same ole routine, awaken by the alarm, get ready, get set, go! Day in and day out, that's what life had begun to feel like. A repeating relay race of get up, get kids up, fix breakfast, prepare lunch, make sure Nick's clothes were pressed, allowing him a few extra minutes to roll that towel under the bathroom door so the smell of marijuana didn't seep through the house. Once everyone else has been taken care of, I would use the last fifteen minutes to get myself together, the second leg of this exhausting race begins! Continuous repetition just like in the movie "Ground Hog Day." I dropped Diamond off at school, then Gem and Onyx at daycare -- miles apart, all before finally hitting that time clock two minutes early with no time for me to exhale. This was my daily routine. Once my nightly routine was complete, and the children were snuggled in their beds, there was just enough time for me to catch up on a few phone conversations. Clearly, my life no longer felt like my own. I didn't even have time to think!!

As I matured, learning to handle all of my responsibilities as a hard-working wife and mother, my older sister Kyndra and

I finally began to develop a relationship. She had been married with children for many years and was able to offer her advice every now and then regarding parenting or marital issues. She was still very religious. I assumed that when she went up to her attic with her Coors lite and weed, her God was okay with that, just as he must've been when she threw her corning ware in the trash because she thought our dying cousin had contaminated it. That all seemed very hypocritical to me. It didn't bother me at all about her addiction. I was used to that behavior. What bothered me was being led to believe or assume that her God approved of the things she was doing wrong. Nick always had a stash, so if she was ever without, I would make sure to supply her need. He had more than enough to share without ever knowing of his generosity. Talking to her became one of my nightly comforts. I didn't follow all of her advice, but I welcomed the opportunity to bond with my sister. She wasn't too much of a gossiper; it was usually all about her God. So, when she told me she saw Nick chillin' a few blocks away on some lady's porch, that definitely raised my antenna!

He specifically left heading to the gym, or so he said, and that was hours ago. I would now start paying more attention to when he left, returned, what he was wearing, and what he smelled like after his so-called workouts. *Oh*, and he'd better be *'stankin'* . Two could play this game, and I knew how to play it much better than him!!!

All the signs were there, but no one said anything. It's always evident when one of the players start being overly nice and doing things out of the norm. Nick was never the type to buy gifts, and he wasn't a very affectionate person either. I guess that all of the cuddling and kissing me on my neck while I was trying to cook, bringing home fresh flowers and cards, was just an admission of guilt. This is a game though, remember, so I'll play along. I'll take all the gifts I can get, as I play my hand. I love fresh flowers, I love affection, and I love cards. I'm not that fond of games; however, like I always said, I had the best instructor - *Hakeem*.

Unfortunately, this went on for quite some time. It finally came to a point where I was just getting tired of pretending everything was ok. Honey always said *you don't share information about your man with anyone*, and that was advice I would cling to. However, after a while, I had to talk to someone. So, I spoke to my sister Kyndra. Well, you know what her solution was - come to church, where she seemed to go every day. I was not sold on that idea, at least not now. I'd take another route.

Our marriage started to feel more like we were friends with benefits. However, the children were happy. I wasn't, but so what. I was used to making sacrifices for my children, this would just be another one. Sometimes I felt like I was Nick's mother too, just like when we were young. Often I would laugh inside, wondering if he thought he was slick and winning at this game. Little did he know I had quit playing .

My mind was contemplating if I could survive at being a single parent, but I couldn't figure it out financially. Herman, with all his advice, should've been telling Nick how to adequately provide for his family because that was the only spicing up we needed at this point. We were still splitting every damn thing down the middle, even the groceries! Nothing irked me more than Nick waiting for me to actually give him half the money right there in the supermarket as if we were not returning to the same household! Nevertheless, having to pay all the bills, including his half, I could not help but feel like I was stuck in this relationship. Trust me, in this game, there are never really any winners!

Chapter 18

❖

I Quit

Balloons, souvenirs, baby carriages squeaking, babies crying, children talking, the smell of manure, and the screeching sound of the trolley slowing up to let us on for the tour of the Turtle Back Zoo – Oh God! This was going to be one long day! Still haven't figured out, for the life of me, why "O" and Herman decided to have the kids' fifth birthday party at the stinking zoo but, there we were. After the tour, we were tucked away in a designated area for parties, but with my dislike for the zoo, combined with my keen sense of smell, I still couldn't wait until this party was over! That is until a scent overwhelmed the place. I can't say I was familiar with the fragrance, but I'll call it Calvin Klein's Obsession for men, and at that very moment, I became obsessed. As I glanced across the room, there he stood, Mr. Suave and Debonair himself, Herman's best friend. I should have known when the aroma filled the room, just who it was coming from -- *"Malcolm."*..

I met him many, many years ago before I even knew Nick existed. I inquired about him, and Herman shut it down! He didn't hesitate to tell me that it was none of my business who this man was! He would make a point that none of his wife's friends would be fucking any of his homeboy's. This time around I had no intention of waiting for Herman's approval. If the opportunity presented itself, this could just be the beginning of an unexpected adventure.

Snap out of it I'd say to myself! Kamara! Look next to you -- on your right is your husband, and on your left there are your three beautiful children. Get your mind out of the gutter!

The party seemed to be dragging along, but now I welcomed the slow pace as Herman and "O" opened each gift and read every card. Some of the children were even getting whiney. Surprisingly, I had blocked out every sound and every smell except the pleasant scent of Obsession. My eyes were fixed on Malcolm who stood out anyway (literally). He had to be about 6'8, lookin' like a lighter, sexier version of Lebron James right down to his long bow legs. I hope Nick wasn't watching me. If he was, it would've been out of the norm. He had to keep a close eye on Onyx, who was our active and friendly child. If he wasn't watching him, Onyx might've wandered off.

Unfortunately, when you learn bad behavior at a young age, it tends to stick with you. When a teenage girl learns "tricks" from a grown ass man, she will always remember them, I sure did. Hakeem's skills had been embedded in me. I realized that when I made eye contact with Malcolm, immediately I winked at him, picked up my fork and slowly and seductively slid a piece of cake in my mouth. I don't even like birthday cake, but he was looking at me, and I wanted him to know I was looking back. My gesture caught him off guard. I'm sure of it because, as if he was nervous, he dropped the handful of cards Herman was passing to him after reading them. I chuckled as he bent down to pick them up and he smirked, in a cute, boyish kind of way.

The weirdest thing happened as we all were making way to our cars. I saw Nick give Malcolm some dap. Did he know him? I hope the hell not! The party was over, but my thoughts would replay again and again, as if I was hitting the rewind button on my VCR.

The hour ride home was serene. The kids had fallen asleep almost instantly. Nick popped in one of his favorite Luther Vandross cassettes and Luther's smooth voice amplified through the speakers...

"The time is right, you hold me tight and loves got me high. Please tell me yes and don't say no, honey not tonight..."

I wanted to hit the off button. My body was here with Nick, but my mind was on the other side of town with Malcolm. Nick had one hand on the steering wheel, the other he placed on top of mine. I thought, oh no honey, not tonight; I closed my eyes and pretended to fall asleep.

Would it be another decade before I'd see Malcolm again?

Chapter 19

❖

90-Day Eviction Notice

Rumor 'round town was that Nick had a girlfriend. I stopped being Sherlock Holmes a long time ago. My focus was on my three children. I did not have the time nor energy to be investigating no man. If he had an outside interest, so be it; I had one too (he just hadn't surfaced yet).

Half the time, I felt like the man in this marriage anyway. When rent was late, I was the one who had to come up with a lie to keep a roof over our heads. All along, he was screwing up the finances and satisfying his marijuana habit that had gotten totally out of control. His habit had even trickled over into the job. One day a co-worker leaned over my desk and whispered, *"Do the kids need anything else?"* I was really puzzled by her question, *Anything Else?* Why did you ask me that? I was so embarrassed when she told me that they had taken up a collection to help Nick with the family hardship! I was appalled, and asked how much did they collect? She walked away without answering, realizing that she had let the cat out of the bag. Needless to say, the family never got any of that collection, and the hardship must have been Nick's lack of marijuana, or whatever he was smoking. When our refrigerator was empty, I came up with a hustle to make sure our children were fed. I could've been selling my tail for all he cared. No matter what, my place of employment would never be involved in any of my personal struggles.

Worrying about how I was going to make ends meet without Nick was no longer a thought. He had two sons he was responsible for, and if he wanted to play hardball, I could file for child support for Diamond too since he adopted her; however, I would never do that. She was Hakeem's responsibility! He was probably out there creating more children for someone else to take care of. I was exhausting myself, continually being the great pretender. Everything in our world was not okay. Simply put, I was miserable!

A month passed since the Turtle Back Zoo birthday bash, yet thoughts were still lingering about Malcolm. Something I had to look forward to now was Herman's upcoming private birthday celebration. Both of us were born in December, the festive time of year. 'Tis the season to be jolly, and oh how I yearned to be jolly!

The time will never be right...

I can still see the reflection of the Christmas tree lights blinking. The children are in bed and should have been asleep, but Onyx was yelling, *"I love you mommy, I love you daddy!"* When neither of us answered, he keeps repeating it. It's as if he knew that night was the night I could no longer avoid what had to be said. I couldn't let this child distract me, finally I yelled back, ***"You better go to sleep!"*** I'd taught my children that every time you say you love someone doesn't mean that person has to reciprocate. We would give him an example of what that meant. Of course, we loved him too, but there was no love in the air at that moment. If he knew how I was feeling, he'd play possum right now! He continued yelling until I finally replied in not such a nice tone, *"I'm coming to your room to show you some tough love!"* Almost Immediately the house was as quiet, as I needed it to be.

Nick was sitting on his side of the bed in his boxers, looking sexy, six-pack in full view on his smooth chocolate skin, but no time for sexy tonight. He knew it; there was a stillness in the air, so I didn't drag this out. I looked him straight in his eyes (never having to utter a single word) -- eyes talk. He said, *"I need some time to find a place."* I responded, *"Okay, will 90 days be enough time?"*; he immediately responded, *"I think so..."*

I turned off the light, with my body the opposite direction of his. I didn't want him to see the tears streaming down my face as they saturated my pillow. I had mixed emotions. It had been twelve years since we started this relationship, and many of those years were great! I wanted to lay on his chest and tell him thank you for the good years, thank you for my beautiful babies, but this just wasn't the time for that. It would only confuse Nick, I didn't want to do that.

As a rule, in the past, we vowed never to go to sleep angry or without saying goodnight.

Tonight, we broke our vow...

Chapter 20

❖

A Night to Remember

"*an I go?*" Those were three words I'd never heard from Nick in the past. I was almost compelled to look behind me to see if someone else was in the house.

I had asked Nick to zip me up as I finished getting dressed for Herman's celebration. If I had enticed him, it definitely was unintentional, we were doing just fine as roommates, counting the days until our freedom. I must admit I did look stunning. I was wearing a black form-fitted satin dress with the back out, hugging my hips giving me just the right amount of sexy. I had gotten a little of my figure back, and what better time than tonight to flaunt it? The silver pumps with my cubic zirconium earrings, necklace and bracelet added that bling I needed to look elegant. My make-up was very natural. Back then, we weren't into upside down Nike sign shaped eyebrows or Elsie the cow lookin' eyelashes (*those things were left on the athletic gear and ice cream packaging*), if you're old enough to know what I'm talking about.

I answered Nick in my new normal way, with my eyes. It certainly cut out the back n' forth chatter that led to unnecessary arguments that wouldn't change a thing! Furthermore, we had three children, and he was their caregiver tonight.

I grabbed my car keys and left.

I took the long drive to their home located in West Orange, NJ, just to unwind and look at all the beautifully decorated neighborhoods. Herman had bought a second home when he decided that he and "O" would give their love another try. It wasn't the same caliber as the mansion in Florida, but it was equally as beautiful. As I approached their home, it reminded me of something from a magazine. The big pine trees were decorated with all blue lights and the house was outlined with the same; it was absolutely mesmerizing. Finally, after sitting in my car, just thinking of all I'd gone through and wondering what would lay ahead for my children and me, I picked up my purse and the little gag gift I'd bought for Herman and began my way up the walkway. I could see the silhouette of a man standing off to the side, and through the huge bay windows, the small gathering of people sitting and standing.

"O" came to the door to greet me, we hugged. Once inside the decorations were more beautiful than outside. Poinsettias, garland, lights, bells, bows, just so festive. As "O" took my coat, a man with a mic recognized me and gestured me to join him with a song. I laughed, asking for a drink to get warmed up. It was none other than NBA world-renowned Chocolate Thunder! We sang our own rendition of the Christmas Song and our small audience was as captivated as I was when that silhouette of a man who was standing outside walked in. It was Malcolm! Whew! He was dressed in a black suit, a light gray shirt, and his multi-colored tie - mostly red. Our outfits matched as if we left the house as a couple (wishful thinking). I had to close my eyes to finish the song.

"They know that Santa's on his way."..I was thinking "Santa" for me just walked in through the front door, and I hoped that he had some goodies...

That was the first of many songs sang that night. There were so many personalities in that house, yet all of us gelled perfectly; we laughed, sipped, ate, played games, danced, told jokes, and listened to Herman who was the biggest joker of us all.

It was clear that Malcolm and I shared a chemistry, but we couldn't make it obvious. We both knew Herman was not in favor of us getting together. We also knew he realized neither of us came with our mates. Malcolm was not married but was very much attached to his live-in girlfriend of five years.

It wasn't like the paparazzi was following us or anything, so we were able to chit chat from time to time at the party. I was able to get my question answered that had been gnawing at me. *"Do you know my husband?"* There was a bit of a pause, then a little wrinkle in his forehead as he responded, *"Husband?" "Yes, I saw you give him dap at the kid's party last month." "Nick???"* Nick from Guyana is **YOUR** husband?' The way he responded I was almost afraid to say yes. I answered, and he laughed! I wasn't feeling his laughter or that moment; it felt awkward until he finally said, *"He's a cool, quiet brother and he can ball. We play ball together on Saturday's."* Malcolm continued, *"I thought his wife would be wearing flowered house dresses, barefoot carrying a bucket on her head." "No, Malcolm."* I explained, *"just because he's a foreigner doesn't mean that. If you knew his culture you'd also know Guyanese women are beautiful."* Maybe we looked too engaged in our conversation because Herman came up to him and said, *"Yo, I need you to help me in this game of basketball trivia."* Needless to say, his interruption was perfectly timed.

Somehow the women had separated from the men, and they were in another room having a 'Waiting to Exhale' party talking about men and all their bullshit! I took my rightful place in the room. Admittedly, I was an expert in this conversation. I damn near had a Ph.D.!

Finally, as the night was winding down, Herman remembered that he'd forgotten to bring out the Dom Perignon Rose' for the toast -- *"Big Willie"* as we sometimes referred to him jokingly. He wasn't about to let that expensive champagne go unopened. All of us gathered in a semi-circle with our host Herman and "O" in the middle. Malcolm conveniently positioned himself behind me. As we raised our glasses, Herman began to speak...

I noticed Malcolm had water and he didn't seem tipsy. I'd already had one too many, but this was the first, and probably last time I'd have the opportunity to drink this expensive champagne, so I kept pouring – *let my cup runneth over.*

Not only was I more than tipsy, but this man was also standing so close to me that my body was all tingly inside (*what a combination, tipsy and tingly*). The lights had been dimmed, and the reflection from the blue lights outside just gave me a romantic feeling almost indescribable.

The Whispers song, "A Special Holiday" echoed throughout the house softly. Joy and gladness were in the air, happy people were everywhere, and it was definitely a very special holiday, and a special night spent with special people. It was a night to remember, a night I wished never had to end.

Chapter 21

❖

Out of the Frying Pan

I'm feeling like the walls are closing in on me. I want Nick gone - out of this house! He had become extremely clingy like a magnet stuck to my ass. This behavior never worked for me. I'm guessing his little fling was over. Not having anyone to vent to at this time made matters even worse. "O" was usually my sounding board, but lately she was under enough pressure of her own. Her first-born son, Adongo, had returned as a teenager after living with his biological dad and grandma for many years. Not only had his stature changed, but he had a whole new attitude as well. He said he was tired of the Georgia heat and wanted to experience the snow and cold weather. Also, he wanted to have some bonding time with his siblings. This man-child was now very opinionated and outspoken. This would be an even bigger problem for "O" and Herman later on down the road.

Regarding my life, I just had to figure things out for myself. In the turmoil of things, I would unintentionally make some bad decisions. *What else is new?* When it came to Malcolm, I lost all logic and common sense. I could not see the forest for the trees. As Honey would say, I was jumping straight out of the frying pan and into the fire, but I liked a little heat, remember?

Without consideration for Nick or my children, I started extending my time spent with Malcolm as if I didn't have a care in the world; sometimes I didn't make it in 'til daylight. As time went on, I started involving my children in this madness by taking them with me, disguising my rendezvous with Malcolm as *family fun*. My plan with getting my children familiar with Malcolm worked like a charm. They loved it! We went to the movies, Six Flags, Dairy Queen and their favorite place, Joe's Pizzeria in New York City. There was no limit to what Malcolm would treat them to. They looked forward to every outing. Somehow, they even knew not to mention these outings to their father. I must admit my behavior had become somewhat reckless -- a way of living I was no longer accustomed to. I'd gone from being selfless to selfish, wanting what I wanted - *Malcolm*. Many times, that meant bypassing anything in my path to be with him. My actions would be those of a woman in love, following her heart and not her head. There would be no more extended living arrangements for Nick and no more discussions! Every reckless jaunt outside of our home finally led to my abrupt decision to move in with Malcolm.

I suppose I was now looking forward to all of my dreams coming true, and of course some of my fantasies. I'd fantasized so much about what I envisioned our uninhibited sex life would be like. Afterall, his kisses alone had me changing my panties on a regular!

Leaving my apartment was bittersweet. We weren't exactly living in luxury like we were at Malcolm's, but it was clean and comfortable. Malcolm's place, on the other hand, was like something from the pages of Better Home & Gardens - every inch was color coordinated and neat as a pin. Before moving in, I was thinking his place would be lacking a woman's touch. Luckily, I wasn't being paid for my thoughts, or I would've been bankrupt. The walls were painted beautiful colors. Some of the wall textures even looked suede with matching draperies and accenting tiebacks. The dining room table was set with gold utensils and plates. There was a burgundy runner with gold trim and matching napkins swirled inside of flute glasses. It was amazingly beautiful! It certainly gave the appearance of a woman's touch or Liberace himself. Another thought of mine was that my children would not be able to move a finger in this house. I was wrong. Malcolm was really good to them and made them feel this was their home too. They seemed to be adjusting well. Malcolm did really well with the children especially considering the fact he only had one daughter, Emerald, who was away at boarding school. We rarely saw her.

For the most part, things were going great between Malcolm and me. He was an excellent provider. He was very focused on education and African heritage. I just loved those qualities about him. Unfortunately, I had not hit the jackpot when it came to sex. There would be no hanging from chandeliers or pole dancing in our bedroom! It turns out that those kisses were just a big ole tease. There were those occasions when I'd try to add a few sparks, but he was resistant most of the time. The one time I pulled out the K-Y jelly and rubber gloves was the time he didn't resist! Now that really raised my eyebrows, and my side eye damn near became crossed. You know what they say, you never really know someone until you live with them, and that just might hold some validity. Malcolm had some peculiar ways, to say the least.

When my hours changed at work, there was nothing I could do except go with the flow that wasn't flowing too well. I reached out to Nick, asking if he could give me a hand with his children; he declined. Considering how I left him, I wasn't surprised by his response, but he was still their father. Nick didn't hesitate at assuming the role of the absentee parent. He became like a ghost in our lives, breezing in on birthdays and Christmas, and if the boys were lucky, there were those random barber shop trips that became a real treat. At this point, I was forced to depend solely on Malcolm. He stepped right in, altering his schedule to care for **my** children. Honey would not be in favor of me leaving my children with Malcolm, no matter how well I thought I knew him; but I was batting zero here, she certainly wasn't altering her schedule to help out with them either.

My Diamond was as smart as a whip and very well versed in what could happen or what should not happen when I wasn't around. I warned her of who was allowed to touch her and where. I trusted Malcolm ninety percent or else I wouldn't have left my children with him; however, I'd never trusted anyone one hundred percent. My daughter knew that if Malcolm made one wrong move, even a gesture that made her or her brothers uncomfortable in any way, that I'd prepare for him his last supper. Getting rid of any man would be that easy. It's true, the way to a man's heart is through his stomach. Have you ever noticed, some men will cheat on us, call us bitches, abuse us, and the list goes on. Then they have the balls to sit at our tables and eat the meals we prepare. ***My, my - and they have the audacity to call us stupid!***

Diamond would never fall asleep until I came home. On my breaks, I would sometimes call to check in on them. On one particular night, she shared with me that all was not well. Just when I thought the ship was sailing smoothly, it may have been slowly sinking...

My thoughts were all over the place, so to get my nerves intact, I made a quick stop at the liquor store to get me a tall can of "Billy Dee Williams" Colt 45. I sat in my car and guzzled it down since there was no drinking at Malcolm's because he was in recovery.

When I walked in, the house was quiet, the boys were asleep. The only sound was coming from the television in our room where Malcolm had fallen asleep too. There sat my Diamond, my little lady, not looking stressed, just relieved her mommy had arrived home safely. The look on her face let me know that whatever she needed to tell me wasn't as bad as the place my thoughts had taken me. Trust me, this 'lil lady was **my** rock; she was wise beyond her years. We hugged, I sat down next to her on the sofa across from the huge aquarium. The gentle sound of the waves, the dim light from the treasure chest, the jewels glistening as it opened and closed, and those beautiful tropical fish floating back and forth. This always seemed to have a calming effect on me. This was a great place to listen.

"Mommy," she began, *"I know you're happy and Malcolm is nice to us, but we miss daddy, and we don't like it here."* She went on to tell me she'd been hiding things, not wanting to make me sad. *"Gem doesn't listen to Malcolm,"* she said. That really surprised me because he was my quiet, laid-back, even-tempered child. It also explained why Malcolm asked me weeks before to have Gem checked for a possible hearing impairment. My son was clearly ignoring him! *There wasn't a thing wrong with this child's hearing!* I'm sure if it. Onyx, who was fully potty trained at a very young age, was now pissing in the bed! How'd I miss that? I never smelled the mattress wreaking of piss. Diamond had been cleaning up behind her brothers to protect them and me. My babies were going through something, yet it had gone unnoticed. At that very moment, my heart stopped! Yes, I was happy, but when you decide to take on the massive responsibility of parenting, it requires sacrifice. Their happiness would have to take precedence over mine.

Here I was again, feeling as if I was lost in the wilderness, alone, not knowing where or who I could turn to. Thankful for having consumed the Colt 45, my facial expression didn't reflect what I was really feeling on the inside. I hugged my daughter and pretended I had it all together, something motherhood taught me to do very well. I assured her that mommy would fix it. Children experience so much when families are separated. Nevertheless, it was my duty to repair what I obviously had broken - *my children.*

Chapter 22

Paving Our Way

Every now and then, I'd run into Barbara in the grocery store or the mall. Now I was feeling really uncomfortable about interacting with her, and honestly didn't want to see her at all, but one day I did. I didn't know whether to just face her or run in the opposite direction. I knew there had been so many rumors floating around about Hakeem and me. Some gossipy women were talking shit about what they would do if some young bitch had a baby by their man! The ones talking most of the BS didn't even have a man!

Lucky for me, a few years earlier I had already told Diamond that she had two fathers. I told her that this would always make her extra special, with double gifts and double love. Unknowingly, that was one of the biggest lies I've ever told. I just knew it was only fair for her to know. I had already heard Barbara found out Hakeem was Diamond's father. Apparently, one of her daughters, spotted us in the mall and went home and told everyone my little girl looked just like her! I am sure that became a huge topic of conversation in their household. I definitely would not have wanted to be a fly on their wall. Up to that time, I thought that Diamond's real identity was the world's best-kept secret. I certainly was not ashamed of having her. She was my most prized possession. It was because of her birth that I had grown into a mature young woman, a woman who had no desire to cause any more pain on another woman. This was one of the reasons I didn't want Barbara to know about Diamond. She had become my friend, and the last thing I wanted was to hurt her in any way. This woman had endured enough pain. I had learned to embrace the sisterhood and what it meant for us as women to build each other up, not tear each other down. Many times, as I traveled down memory lane I didn't like myself, especially when I thought of all the things I allowed Hakeem to coerce me into doing; I felt ashamed. I became an accomplice in all the ways he had stolen from Barbara's heart, and in all the ways he tried to demean her and strip her of her dignity. As if I was innocent, I hid behind the fact that I was a young girl, but if there was ever a court of love, my age wouldn't have made me any less guilty of the crime. It was time for me to right my wrongs, if that was possible.

I finally reached out to Barbara to give her a call, I guess it was just fate that this happen. With a tremble in my voice, I hardly knew where to begin. Barbara made it easy. She was kind, loving, mild-mannered, understanding and forgiving beyond measure to not only me, but also her husband. This woman was, and still is a rare individual -- not too many people in this world are like her. To this day, I still don't know why Hakeem was never satisfied in their relationship. I guess I will never know.

Barbara even suggested that we get together with Diamond a few times to ensure that she was comfortable with them before she started visiting without me. We made this decision without Hakeem; we didn't need him anyway? As a matter of fact, we didn't even mention his name. Unbelievably, we were able to bond in a way that I am unable to describe, it was so heartfelt. From that point on, our journey as a blended family began. We got off to a great start. When Diamond would go spend weekends with her extended family, her brothers would spend time with their auntie Kyndra. This would give everyone an outlet, a happy one, I hoped. Diamond would always come home with a happy story about her sisters and her *"bonus mom."* She was the oldest sibling in our house, and the youngest in theirs. Gem and Onyx had their happy stories too -- going to church and eating auntie Kyndra's macaroni and cheese that they thought was to die for. Unfortunately, what started out so great came to an end one Sunday evening when Diamond came home nearly in tears.

While me, Barbara, and the kids were having our bonded family moments, Hakeem was in rehab recovering from his misuse of drugs and alcohol. Somehow he learned about Diamond's weekend visits and signed himself out of the rehab center against medical advice. I'm certain his intentions were sincere, he wanted to see Diamond too. However, this would be his biggest mistake by far. Perhaps it was nerves or even anxiety that caused him to make a pit stop at the liquor store on the way to meet her. A drunk man is definitely not the first impression you want to leave with someone, especially not your princess. She was not accustomed to the behavior she witnessed as he staggered towards her with his hands outstretched, as if he wanted a hug. He slurred, *"You're so pretty."* Diamond backed away with a look of fear. Immediately, Hakeem looked sad. He was never good at being rejected. The look of sadness quickly turned into a look of rage! Many years had passed since I'd seen that look, but as Diamond described it, I could also see it so clearly. What followed was very ugly -- the raging bull emerged, shouting and shoving! All of this was directed at Barbara as if they were the only two people in the house. He was ranting as if there was some kind of conspiracy going on, with everyone getting to love on his baby girl and he couldn't! He turned abruptly, looked at Barbara and yelled, *"If it weren't for me, she wouldn't be here in the first place!"* The rock had already been thrown, and with a quick glance at Diamond, Hakeem realized the fear his words and actions had imposed on her. For a split second, he seemed to empathize. He quickly pushed Barbara into their bedroom as if privacy would make this nightmare go away, but the only thing that would go away would be his daughter, and she would be gone for a very long time.

Diamond was mortified, looking sad and bewildered as we sat in our favorite room by the aquarium, hoping to add some tranquility to all the chaos. She continued sharing how she had been traumatized. Finally, she lay in my arms and dropped the tears she'd been holding back *"Mommy, "I never want to see that drunk man again, I want my Daddy!"*

I had failed miserably at my quest to make sure she was happy in her new blended family. Her heart was broken, and now mine was too.

Chapter 23

❖

From the Palace to the Pigpen

I couldn't understand, for the life of me, why Malcolm had not been in favor of the children spending weekends away. He had rarely seen the one daughter he had, yet at times, he seemed obsessed with having my children around.

Our relationship wasn't free from the average ups and downs, but for the most part, it was okay. Secretly, I was fighting my own internal battle, trying not to let the lack of sexual explosions or Malcolm's weird desire to enter from the *back door* instead of the *front door*, overrule my decision to move on. Sometimes practicing abstinence with him and using my sexual toys without him was much more gratifying.

Every now and then, Malcolm would spend weekends away, claiming that he was caring for his grandparents who were not only aging, but ailing as well. Since we met, he had always been close to them. While I did have my suspicions as to why the entire weekend was needed, I was not going to waste my thoughts on something so trivial. I had much bigger fish to fry -- caring for my children and trying to create a happy place for them.

Whenever Malcolm wasn't home, my curiosity got the best of me when the phone would constantly ring from his office, which was more like a library. This was actually the dark room where he stored and watched his private videos – his equivalent of a modern-day *"man cave."* It went without saying that this space was off limits. I would hear that beep, then a click, and my ear was at the door like a magnet, listening to those messages. He could have, at least, turned the sound down; men ain't never been slicker than women. We would have at least done that, and hell, probably would have unplugged that answering machine and took it with us. Now it rang so much, I should have just pulled up a chair and waited for the next ring! Surely, this was none of my business; but it was just what I needed to hear... *"Malcolm, where are you? This is me, BJ. I'm still here waiting at the train station for you to pick me up. Where to this time? Poconos? Hurry, it's cold, love you..."*

Of course, I first tried to rationalize these cryptic messages, knowing he was in recovery and his support group members might check on him now and then; ***Umm...*** *'the Poconos and where to this time'* definitely raised a **FLAMING** red flag! **BJ?** *Who in the hell was he, "Bruce Jenner?"*

I never confronted Malcolm about these weird voice messages because I really had no business listening to them. In addition to that, part of me didn't even want to have that conversation for fear of what I may learn; If he tried to lie, I would know instantly. I just wasn't ready to deal with him, BJ, the back door, the front door or the damn Poconos! I had enough going on. It was hard enough trying to find the words to tell him that my children and I were going to move.

Nothing I could say would make him understand my reason for leaving. He was a great provider, and had a beautiful home. I dare not mention my sexual frustrations; surely, he wouldn't understand that either. As far as he was concerned, he was putting it down, handling his business!

So, I began my search for an affordable place to reside, a search that, with my budget and my less than perfect credit, would send me right to the hood! Finally, after three months of being rejected, and Malcolm's bad attitude, I received a *"yes, you can move in."* By now, there was no turning back.

The *straw that broke the camel's back* was when Onyx gave me the scare of a lifetime! Diamond and Gem ran into our room with Onyx fanning his mouth! He told us he drank rubbing alcohol! He was looking somewhat lethargic. In a panic, I called 911 while Malcolm called poison control. They told us to go to the ER. While there, Onyx asked a question, *"Is my daddy here?"* I then realized his reasoning as a child. This was the only plan he could think of to be reunited with his dad, it worked. Nick came, and suddenly Onyx felt better. I then had to hear all the backlash from the deadbeat dad! If there was any alcohol nearby, I would've thrown it in Nick's eyes! Who was he to be questioning my parenting?

I was so upset with Onyx, but he was just a kid. I knew I had to move on, not for me, but for my children. Malcolm was not hearing it, even if I thought for a second about changing my mind. His weekend rendezvous had gotten worse, and now I was not even privileged to the lies he used to tell me about caring for the grandparents. He would pack his bags and just go. He was hurt, and hurt people hurt people. One great thing that came out of this was that I no longer had to *"pick up the soap"* I guess BJ was doing that!!

Here we are with not even enough stuff to fill up our one-bedroom apartment. Yep, you heard me, our one bedroom; but we were together -- four of us; this could only make us closer. My children would now have my undivided attention -- no Malcolm!

Nick would stop by occasionally after the Onyx scare. He made certain, it was before the sun went down because even with that big club on his car, he didn't want to risk it being stolen. I'm guessing that Nick thought he was at the top of his game and it felt good to be looking down on me. He now had a Peugeot. I must admit, it was nice. If I could shun my responsibilities, and not consider my children, I'd have nice things too. This wasn't how I was used to living either, but I was doing the best I could with what I had. Being responsible came first, holding my family down, and not parading around town in some expensive car! That's what real parent's do. Hopefully, this wouldn't last too long for us, but when I tell you we had gone from *the palace to the pigpen,* I meant that literally.

When I signed the short-term lease, the building looked pretty good. Once we moved in, looks became deceiving. In the evenings, when we returned from work and school, there were so many people sitting on the steps. We had to maneuver ourselves around the people, beer cans and the stench of smoke, just to get into our apartment. This was almost unbearable. Emptying the trash was like a visit to Jurassic Park. There were so many stray dogs and cats waiting to devour whatever was in the garbage. The mice sang lullabies in the walls at night. I was so afraid, but every day, I worked extra hard, trying to be the brave parent. My smiles were brighter, and my hugs were tighter. I was winning at being the great pretender; my children seemed to be at a happy place - mission accomplished.

While my children slept, I watched over them like a pit bull with the music trying to drown out the sound of the mice scurrying inside the walls. I was making myself sick. I was drained from exhaustion. Of all people, I had even lost my appetite.

Malcolm and I would still talk, but it was nothing like it used to be. Nick would do his drive-byes, and I even accepted a visit or two from Hakeem. I was desperate for company! I felt like I had hit rock bottom. I was in the gutter, wondering how I was going to get out...

There were times I certainly wished I could adopt the same mentality as the deadbeat dads in my life. Doing the best that I could, just did not seem good enough! This single parenting was not as easy as it looked. I was overwhelmed, wishing I could throw in the towel too!

Chapter 24

❖

From Bad to Worse

I had to go cry on my sister's shoulders. That was extremely hard for me. I wasn't a visible crier, all my tears were shed on the inside, and for fear of what she might say, spilling my guts to her was definitely a clear sign I was at my lowest. She welcomed me, and we went to her place of solitude, her attic. She reached for my hands and began to pray. As she continued, her words started running together as she began to cry. Even though I didn't have a clue what she was saying, it was a great time for me to join her by shedding more tears. I needed to get it out!! At the end of her chanting, she said, *In Jesus' name, Amen.* I said nothing. She hugged me tightly, then released me and placed her hand on my tummy. There was a little pouch that I hadn't noticed – *"Is something in the oven girl?"* Immediately, I said, *"Better not be."* We talked for more than an hour. She finally got me to agree to visit her church. I didn't say when, but I promised that I would. As we conversed, I wasn't entirely focused on her advice; my mind kept shifting to the pouch in my lap. For the past several months I'd been too stressed to pay attention to anything other than my children and making ends meet.

When I made it back to the pigpen, I went straight for the box that I still hadn't unpacked marked "Bathroom." There they were my case of Stay-Free Maxi Pads untouched.

I had better visit Kyndra's church before I took a pregnancy test! All she talked about was her Savior and getting saved. Maybe he could save me from having another mouth to feed!!

You have no idea how high my anxiety level was with just the thought of being pregnant. I had to purchase the pregnancy test before ever making it to church.

The plus sign results meant one more mouth to feed, one more person to make sacrifices for, and one more person to struggle to raise as a single parent. I prayed that this wouldn't be the case.

How was I going to break the news to Malcolm? Would he be happy? He only had one child, and she was now well into her teens. Perhaps this will be a son, every man wants a son (right?). He loved my children, surely he would welcome his own. Every question I asked, I answered. My mind was like a maze.

When I finally got up the nerve to tell Malcolm, my children were lucky that I hadn't inherited the mental illness gene from Honey; otherwise, I would have ended up on the window ledge ready to jump! He was as cold as ice and straight to the point. He would not leave me guessing how he felt. He told me to make an appointment at the nearest abortion clinic and let him know the cost! He added that if I thought for a second about having this child, then I should think again! He emphatically stated if I didn't do as he instructed, I would be raising this child alone, and that he promised. I never uttered a word but was tempted to leave him hanging on the other end with just the hum of a dial tone in his ear. There are no words to explain how my heart hurt that day. I don't know what I was expecting, but it wasn't that.

So, I complied with his request the very next day and scheduled an appointment to have an abortion. Malcolm remained true to his word. He bought the entire payment with a little extra and noted that the excess was for my taxi there and back. I suppose cab fare was his show of compassion. When he walked away, I thought of the day I met him -- the instant attraction, my broken marriage, Nick's broken heart, Hakeem and the games he taught me that I mastered, and Barbara's broken heart. Could this all be part of my reaping what I had sown? Was this my turn to join the broken hearts club? I thought of the butterflies I felt and how now I just felt sick! As he walked away, there even seemed to be a difference in the way he walked, like a twitch. **Bastard!** For a second, I hated him!!! I now had a clearer understanding of what the lyrics meant in the hit song of the seventies, *"It's A Thin Line Between Love and Hate."* I was trying hard not to throw a can or anything to hit him in the back of his big ass head!

Two weeks later, there I was at the abortion clinic. I had to pull a number from this machine and wait to be called as if I was in some type of slaughterhouse. I was number twenty-three. Kyndra was very supportive of my decision to have an abortion or rather, Malcolm's insistence that I do this. When I began to have doubts and mixed feelings, Kyndra reminded me of how hard things were and how they'd get even worse with another child. Looking back, how in the hell would she know? She had a husband, a house, well-rounded children; and oh, let's not leave out her Savior! I wondered why she didn't mention him this time and how he could *"Save my unborn child and me"* wouldn't that be a better option than getting my child vacuumed out of me (truly that's all an abortion is), *right?* It had been well past three months since I had my cycle now that I'd taken the time to focus and calculate. Did her Savior allow murder or was this different since I had never met him or her? By now, this place is packed to standing room only. They have just called number twenty, so it's almost my turn. I turn to the young lady sitting next to me, who I'm sure didn't feel like talking; who would in this atmosphere? Everyone is in here for the same thing. I take my chances and start the conversation anyway.

I started with a weak hello, just to check her vibe; she could probably see the look of apprehension (or fear) on my face. She responded, "Hey." I asked, " *Have you ever been to this place before?*" Her very lackadaisical response was, *"Yes, three times"* (it became obvious that abortions were her form of birth control). She continued by saying, *"If you're having second thoughts lady, this isn't the place for you."* Another number was called, and she left. There was a phone booth in front of me that seemed to be calling my name. I placed a collect call to Honey because I didn't have enough coins. I burst into tears, something I'd been doing on a regular since I got this news. Honey screamed, ***"What's wrong?"*** I told her all I had been going through fighting my way through this jungle, and what bought me to where I was at that moment. She shared with me about her experiences with pregnancies, single parenting, and fears she overcame as she raised us. She encouraged me to leave the slaughterhouse, hold my head up high as she did, and have my baby; everything would be ok. In my opinion, a mother is always right in her child's eyes, even once they've reached adulthood.

"Number twenty-three!" , I heard someone yell. I looked back, then looked at the piece of paper in my hand with the big number twenty-three stamped on it; I crumbled it and walked out...

As I walked out, I could still hear Honey, as I always do and as I always will. I held my head up, I rubbed my pouch, and I apologized to my unborn child for having a weak moment. I promised to do all within my power to have a healthy pregnancy and to get him or her here. I also beat myself up, wondering how I could ever allow anyone to influence me even to entertain the thought of committing murder because that's what I believe an abortion is.

Did I need a man to help me raise these children? *"No!"* Did I want one? *"Yes!"* I believed that the family unit should include a man, woman, and child (ren); but, the more I thought about it, the more complicated it became.

I didn't need Malcolm, he wasn't a man! After all, a real man opens the door for his lady - *the front door.*

Much later in the day, my phone rang several times; each time I was reluctant to answer it. There were a select few who knew my daily routine. I really wasn't in the mood for possibly being interrogated. I knew that eventually, I'd have to talk. The first caller was Kyndra. She was disappointed in the decision I had made, but *now* she decided to offer her Savior. With my eyes rolled as far to the back of my head as they could go, I listened.

Just before midnight, I received my last call, it was Malcolm. "Are you ok," he asked, as if he really gave a damn. *"How'd everything go?"* My response, *"I couldn't do it, I couldn't kill my baby!"* The tone of his voice totally changed as he continued to speak, *"Oh really Kamara, I hope that you remember my promise!"* And without hardly taking a breath, he followed with, *"And where's my fucking money!"* I responded very calmly, (over the years I'd learned that this really pisses people off) *"I'm keeping your money Malcolm, and it'll be applied to your first child support payment. Now, let me make **YOU** a promise cupcake, and this I'll guarantee, I will see you in court in the very near future. Rest easy."*

Chapter 25

❖

Escaping the Jungle

At my dwelling on South Arlington Avenue in East Orange, New Jersey, the place I would never learn to call home, the happenings seemed to always occur during the wee hours of the morning. No matter how long I lived there I never slept peacefully, and one eye was always open to guard my children.

Out of nowhere came a loud banging on our door! I jumped up, didn't have to run to gather the children because we all slept in the same room. A loud voice was yelling, *"fire, fire, get out, get out!!! Everyone must evacuate the building!!!"* I was in a panic as Diamond, with the level head, started gathering coats and telling her brothers to get their shoes on. *Just who was the mother here?* I'm now almost nine months pregnant and can barely walk, so running for my life would feel like a marathon achievement. I opened the door, and the smoke was so thick, visibility was poor. I could hear the crackling sounds of fire, but I did not see any flames. People were racing down the stairs damn near stampeding over one another. Diamond was holding Onyx, and thankfully a man scooped him right out of her arms; it was clear she was struggling. We all made it out safely. It was hard to believe so many families were housed in this deplorable apartment building. It was late December with frigid temperatures, and our car didn't have any heat. The wait for the firemen to call all clear seemed like an eternity. My face, hands, and feet felt like ice cubes *(if you've ever felt the winters up north, you know exactly what I mean)*, but it beat the odds -- It was either freeze or burn to a crisp.

"All clear! All clear!", I heard the fireman yell. To be honest, I was hoping the damn building burned down to the ground. I was hesitant to go back in. My children were looking at me with tears in their eyes, or maybe that was a glassy look because they were cold! I knew we had to go back in. The smell of smoke was breathtaking, and the water damage throughout the building was only going to be the breeding ground for more roaches, rats, and who knows what else. At that very moment, I knew we had to escape from this jungle; I just didn't have a plan.

The following month my baby was born, another son. Caz was right there by my side. If it wasn't for the sisterhood I don't know where I'd be, or if I'd even exist. The contractions started, I called her, and she was there faster than an ambulance. The delivery was almost effortless; he came within an hour of my arrival at the hospital. I remember the labor and delivery unit was packed that day. The staff at Beth Israel Hospital seemed only focused on making room for the next delivery. Shortly after I delivered him, the nurse asked if I felt up to walking to my room? However, she failed to tell me that the room was on another wing of the facility. I found myself, ass out, pushing my intravenous, pole stepping over blood mixed with betadine.

Was there anything else that could add to the unpleasant events in my life during this time? I thought of the saying, what doesn't kill you will make you stronger; well I must've been "The Hulk." I made it to the room with double beds thankful no one else was there yet. I heard a baby screaming as if someone was torturing it. The nurse reached for my armband, checked it, then compared it with the screaming infant. She said, *"This one belongs to you, and he has some set of lungs; who has the temper in the family?"* I slowly sat down on the edge of the bed as my baby continued to scream. I looked at him, I looked at me, and I looked at the window. Finally, the sadness that I was holding inside escaped through my eyes; I cried too. I picked him up, and I immediately was reminded of all I had sacrificed to get him here. I had even quit my job of fifteen years to save face for Nick. I asked myself, was it all worth it, and a little voice inside of me answered, *"yes it was."* I'd never regret not answering the call for number twenty-three.

I didn't even have a name for my little cry baby. Gem told me about a name of his classmate that he liked, Malachite. I looked up the meaning. It's action to protect you from negative energies is one of its most powerful attributes. It aids creativity, enhances the development of your intuition. It is a strong stone for the heart, both the physical heart and to aid your healing emotionally. I absolutely loved the meaning. I thanked his big brother for the name, and so it was.

When we were discharged from the hospital, Caz was right there to pick us up. She said we were not returning to the jungle, she had rearranged some things in her apartment and was taking us home with her. My heart was filled with gratitude. I was overwhelmed by her act of kindness. Her actions displayed the true meaning of friendship, sacrifice, empathy and the love I was so in need of.

Chapter 26

---❖---

Praise Tabernacle

After salvaging what I could from, what I'd like to refer to as, the jungle, I was beyond thankful to Caz that I would never have to return there again. When it was time for me to seek employment, Caz suggested that I return to University Hospital. She also said, Nick had pictures of the children plastered around his cubical, and when conversing with his co-workers, everyone thought he deserved the title as father of the year! If I had returned to that facility, I would've definitely been forced to rain on his parade. I decided to let Nick continue pretending to be something he was not - an amazing father.

When Malachite, at two months old, was still exercising those good set of lungs, he was causing me to use mine. I wondered had Malcolm been on crack and concealed that too, I was in a hurry to find a job and a babysitter! Still looking pregnant and with milk leaking from my breast (a girdle and breast pads took care of that), I heeded the call to seek employment.

I found a job at a small private hospital on the other side of town in the suburbs. It was nothing like where I'd come from. I didn't know anyone, which made it a great place to start anew. I was feeling much better about myself and the direction my life was heading. Now would be the perfect time for me to visit Kyndra's church, "Praise Tabernacle."

Praise Tabernacle was nothing I could've ever imagined. We walked into the sounds of drums, tambourines, guitars, keyboards, and singing! A few ladies were dancing up front with hats on that looked more like lampshades. This was nothing like what I remembered at my grandmother's church with the crushed-up crackers and doll-size cups of juice. Seems like I should've visited a long time ago, they might be serving biscuits and Manischewitz wine on first Sundays.

"I don't know what you came to do, I don't know what you came to do, I came to praise the Lord."..those were the lyrics coming from their mouths. The sounds and energy prompted me to start clapping and singing along. I came to praise him too, whoever He was. Now, this was a party I intended to come back to. The ladies standing in the aisles wearing what looked like nursing uniforms even took Malachite's crybaby self off of my hands! Yes!!! This was my kinda party! I came to praise the Lord, and we would surely be coming back.

All those conversations that Kyndra and I had about my visiting her church, and she never spoke of the fun, only about her Savior whom I hadn't met yet. I wouldn't need any more invitations; some Sundays we arrived before her. I looked forward to it. It became second nature to me. It wouldn't be long before Caz and "O" would join me to see what all the hype was about.

If I ever had to describe the church, it would come pretty close to how I imagine the White House. There was a set routine on Sundays, and now I knew it step by step. There was the pastor (who they treated like the POTUS), and his wife who was referred to as the First Lady. The pastor would be announced, and before entering from a side door with secret service agents (the Armor Bearers), we were all asked to stand and give him a hand clap of praise! Don't know why we were praising him, but

I fell right in line, just like everyone else. I was proud to be a part of the Praise Tabernacle family. The way Kyndra used to badger me about visiting, I was now doing the same to others. Every Sunday there would be another added to our numbers, which seemed to be the goal. I won favor with the pastor and first lady because I would always bring a guest or two. I didn't know then, but later on, I realized this also meant a more substantial amount of money in the collection plates.

Barbara and I never lost contact, even though Diamond never returned after the night she was traumatized at their house. Occasionally, she would meet up with her extended family at Hakeem's mom's place, a safe place minus the drama. I reached out to Barbara and invited her to Praise Tabernacle. She was not able to attend due to her busy schedule supporting her man. Hakeem had gotten himself together and was no longer a Muslim and was now an ordained minister of the gospel. Barbara remained by his side, a true ride or die chick. They were traveling a lot and contemplating relocating to Georgia to start their own ministry. Hakeem loved traveling, loved people and loved talking. People gravitated towards him, so I could see him being a preacher, and the more I got acclimated to the church scene, the more I could see it.

I was at the church so much now, but I still hadn't quite brushed elbows with the Savior. Perhaps I was missing something or just too involved with everything else! I was at the church six days a week. I had become a real social butterfly. Once I joined, I was privy to much more than I ever knew existed. There was a committee for cleaning the church, selling dinners, organizing concerts and fashion shows, you name it, we had it! The Fox Theater probably had fewer bookings than us.

Then finally there were the sermons, the real reason we were in attendance -- to get that spiritual food I was told. Hell, I was there for the party, and the soul food -- perhaps my distraction by the praise party was keeping me from what I really needed. The cooks didn't play down in the church basement! There was a Thanksgiving menu prepared **every** Sunday – this was the temptation that was hardest to resist.

The interlude before the preaching had more marches than the Civil Rights movement! There was a march for the praise team, a march for the choir, a march for the benevolent offering, then the silver offering; and finally, there was the tither's march, where the line grew very long, and you were ridiculed if you were not joining that line. "O" would line up right behind me and after church, she would ask me, *"Are you really putting ten percent of your income in that envelope?"* I said, *"Yes, aren't you?"* She had me almost peeing on myself from laughing so hard! *"**Hell no!**"* I just get in line because he makes the people who don't join the line feel guilty or cheap -- especially when he quotes the scripture:

Malachi 3:8 -18 (KJV) *"Will a man rob God?"* Yet, ye have robbed me. *But ye say, wherein have we robbed thee?* In tithes and offerings.

"O" then said *"Girl, yet ye have robbed me?"* -- Me who?!, Your *bootleg preacher?, she said" "Kamara, he's robbing you blind, and you have all of these kids to take care of. I put a damn dollar in that envelope! That's all I had to give! God knows my heart. Furthermore, what are you paying for? Half the time we don't have a clue what he's preaching about."* "O" was partially right, but I didn't feel like I was being robbed. We had a nice clean church to party in, a built-in babysitter and Sunday dinner for a family of five; therefore, no matter what I was tithing, it was worth it.

The major problem I had with the preaching was that I never really understood what the preacher was saying. He would read a few scriptures from the Bible then title it; midway into his sermon. His voice changed, it became really raspy! He began sweating profusely like a man about to have a heart or asthma attack. His breathing scared me until one of the ladies dressed in the nursing attire (the ushers) calmly handed him a handkerchief and a glass of water. He wiped his forehead, sipped the water, and continued with his obvious performance. How could anyone get a message out of that? "O" would come just to make jokes and at times, to criticize. I remember her saying, *"He couldn't preach his way out of a paper bag!"*

Chapter 27

❖

Wolves in Sheep's Clothing

I started paying more attention to what he was saying, rather than what he was doing. One evening, during Bible study, Pastor mentioned that some of us needed to tell him what we were believing God for. He said, "Many of our prayers wouldn't make it up to Him." He'd have to go to God on our behalf only that didn't apply to the members who had the gift of giving -- meaning, when church dismissed you had nothing left, not even a coin! There's a time that remains vivid in my mind when I probably was down to my last ten dollars, so I didn't join any marches other than the tithers' march on that day. Like "O" said, pastor tended to make you feel guilty. He went on to say that *"God knows when you're down to your last; Luke 6:38 (KJV) tells us to give (our last), and it shall be given unto us, pressed down, shaken together and running over;"* it will be poured into our laps! I listened, and I gave my last ten dollars, knowing this was my baby's diaper money! The only thing that was poured into my lap was Malachite's urine from his saturated pamper. As I left the church that night, I prayed the only way I knew how. I let God know I had given from my heart and my baby had no more pampers. Pastor's son Drake was standing at the door shaking hands as we departed. When my turn came, I reached to shake his hand, but this shake was different; It almost felt erotic as he glided his hand across mine. When I opened my hand, there was a twenty-dollar bill in it. First, I thought there is a God! Secondly, I wondered why did Drake just give me money? Was it the big wet spot on the front of my dress? Had he heard me tell "O" I needed Pampers, or was he tuned in to my spirit? I wanted to turn back and say thank you, but my better judgment told me to keep walking.

Kyndra was so devoted to Praise Tabernacle and the first family. It struck me really strange when she suddenly took ill and was admitted into the hospital. Pastor didn't visit her. When I confronted him, he told me it was not a Pastor's place to visit women. I didn't understand his response, especially when he and I were having our long conversations face to face and on the phone, all the time. Weren't those visits? Besides that, more than half of his parishioners were women! My daddy used to tell me this wasn't normal. As far I was concerned, it was. Our church family was very close-knit. The congregation was small, about forty members on a crowded day. We were like his daughters. What was abnormal about a spiritual father chatting with his daughters (*except some of our chats were outside of the spiritual scope*)? I dare not tell my daddy that!

Things seemed different when Kyndra returned to church a couple months later. She was distant and not quite so hands-on like she was before her hospitalization. Our Associate Pastor had recently left the church saying God called her to start a ministry of her own. Pastor reluctantly gave her his blessing; he didn't really seem sincere. Perhaps that was because when she left, many members left with her, which meant many more dollars left too. Whisperers were saying Kyndra was leaving as well. She was my sister, and she didn't tell me; therefore, I just chalked that up as a rumor.

Every once in a blue moon, Pastor would preach a sermon that I understood. He would get through it without all the huffing and puffing! Those were the times I left the church spiritually fed, while the majority of others were complaining and dissatisfied. If the singing didn't move them to swollen eyes, and Pastor didn't get to the part which always mimicked the onset of an asthma attack, these people were not moved. It was only during those theatrics that they spoke of Pastor being used by God! My people were in love with performances, I wasn't. One of his sermons was entitled "God's Watching", he referenced from the book of Proverbs: "The Lord sees everything you do. He watches where you go. An evil man will be caught in his evil ways..." This sermon was the breaking point for me. There were many times when I referred to that scripture again and again, right there in the church. I was slowly learning that everyone who hollered *"Hallelujah"* was not "Holy." It was as if God was making the messages simple just for me to understand, to see the light in the midst of darkness. He knew what I needed, it was just taking me some time, some more heartbreaks, some more wolves in sheep's clothing before I'd finally get to where He wanted me to be. *God is patient...*

God will meet us wherever we are, I'm thankful for that. He is watching. He truly chastens those that he loves. He knows the wolves, he knows the sheep, there are no disguises, no mask that God cannot remove or see through. God didn't need those performances. He wasn't giving out any Oscars or Grammys! He was saving souls, mending hearts, and the most significant part was, He didn't mind digging through all the layers of muck and mire to rescue the little-lost girl who was trapped inside of me.

It became evident, Pastor, on several occasions certainly did not practice what he preached, and his son Drake, the young man who slipped me the twenty-dollar bill, turned out not to be much of a saint either. For some reason, I gave him the benefit of the doubt, thinking he must've been in tune with my spirit. I refused to allow my thoughts to go in any other direction. After all, Drake was Pastor's right-hand man. He was the Sunday school teacher, the choir director, and the youth minister, a part of the elite amongst the clergy. He was also very well groomed, a quality I would always find attractive in a man. Nothing was ever out of place on him even that wet look, "soul glow" Jheri curl – so evenly lined up with that one Michael Jackson curl right in the front of his forehead. Brother "D" is what the youth called him. To me, he wasn't too far in age from the youth he was leading. I was eight years his senior, but he was much wiser than me in a biblical sense -- very well rounded with the church flow of things.

I decided to join the choir since the Associate Pastor left and several choir members left with her. She was a spirit-filled, very respected woman that we all loved. It was no surprise that almost half the church followed her. She came from a family of southern preachers, and on the Sunday's Pastor would allow her to teach (because that's definitely what she did). There was always standing room only. Every pew was filled. Even "O" listened to her very intently. At times Pastor seemed jealous. The Praise Tabernacle family definitely suffered a loss when she left, but no one spoke of it as we pulled together and continued our praise without her and those that went with her.

I was no stranger to recognizing the sly, the slick, and the wicked outside of the church, but I was still wet behind the ears within the church. Therefore, I let my guard down and was far too trusting when I shouldn't have been. Brother "D" and I were forced to work together since I joined the choir. He was giving me voice lessons as he built my confidence to become one of his lead vocalists. During our extended rehearsals, he always looked at me straight in the eyes. As we practiced a duet, he held both my hands to help me unwind and lose my nervousness. He was excellent at what he did, and we became the dynamic duo, belting out hits originally sang by BeeBee and CeeCee Winans. We also bought the *"cha-ching"* back into the church. "D & K" were the headliners on the church bulletin. He sat at the baby grand piano as I leaned on it. He was super talented and could play any song just by listening to it, no sheet music required. He bought out the best in me vocally. I felt like a celebrity. We would even coordinate our clothing the night before we *performed* (ministered in music, that is).

Pastor knew a lot of people, many of whom had radio stations and access to production companies. This opened many doors in the gospel world for me that I'd never even dreamed of. Drake was no stranger to this world either. He would spend quality time with me, touching my stomach, teaching me to hold it in and sing from my diaphragm. Some nights, he would come to my apartment for us to practice so my children could be home and in their beds at a reasonable hour. I had since moved from Caz's place to a really nice place of my own in Union, nearer to my job.

One night there was a terrible storm. Drake lived on the other side of town. He was well into his twenties, but he still lived with his parents. It was too dangerous for him to leave. I heard him make a phone call to let his father, our pastor, know he would be staying with me for the night. Surprisingly, there was no resistance from our pastor. I even heard a chuckle (*wasn't sure what that was all about*). Knowing Pastor the way I did, gave me a vibe that he was not acting as a pastor during this brief phone call, but as proud, puffed up father. I imagined him giving Drake a pat on the back for being stuck at the right place -- my place

-- at the right time. I offered him my room, and I'd sleep on my couch. I needed to be in full view, just in case any of my children awakened. Hopefully, the storm would end, and he would be dismissed before then. We sat in my room and talked like we did most nights on the phone, but in person was different. Drake was cocky and extremely confident about everything! When he realized the storm wasn't letting up, he took it upon himself to remove BeeBee and CeeCee from my CD player and replaced it with Tevin Campbell, *"Tell Me What You Want Me to Do."* I was sitting on the sofa in my room. He reached for my hands the same way he did when he was connecting with me to sing our duets. This time it was different though; I stood up. He then led me just as he confidently leads the youth at our church. He guided me, pressing his body up against mine as if we were doing the old people's two-step. He probably thought that was all I knew how to do. I was trying not to look at him. He was so confident, and I was so vulnerable. He told me that as long as we asked for God's forgiveness for of all our sins, known and unknown, we would be forgiven, regardless to what we had done (*or were planning to do*).

He started singing the lyrics to the song coming from the CD, and boy, could he sing! His voice sounded like Fred Hammond, but better.

Drake started singing: *"It hurts me deep inside when I see you cryin'. Whatever's wrong, I'll make it right. Tell me what you want me to do. My love is always here for you..."*

We had so much fun that night that we hadn't noticed when the storm stopped raging. We danced to the beat of our own music, and it took my breath away. Hopefully, God wasn't watching *EVERYTHING*. I didn't know about Drake and his twisted philosophy, but I sure hoped God already left the room.

Our closeness had become quite obvious and people were starting to talk. *What else is new?* Perhaps there was a difference in our aura. To us, nothing changed. There was so much judgment going on in the church, I hadn't figured out how the sinners were any different from the so-called Christian's. At least in the *secular world* (as they put it), the sinners kept it real.

My sister was looking for an excuse to leave the church; she was no longer happy there. She told me how things had changed, and people she thought were real over the years, had now been revealed to her as fake and phony! I knew she was saddened after her stay in the hospital, but she used Drake and me as a reason for her departure. I assume placing the blame on us made her feel justified. Her spoiled brat sister, stirring up gossip and getting all the attention (*again*), just like when we were little girls. It was not long before Kyndra and her family left Praise Tabernacle. They joined the former associate pastor at her church that I'd heard was doing very well. Their congregation had already outnumbered ours with both men and women. It seemed so competitive amongst the churches. Who had the most members, who sang the best, who preached the best, who had the biggest damn lampshade on their head? It probably was easier to find God in the club!

"The Wounded Soldiers Ministry" -- Where wounded souls are healed on this battlefield called life.

This was what the banner read outside of the former associate, now pastor's church.

It was itching at me to sneak in a visit. The name of the church was quite alluring.

I was so hurt when Kyndra said to me that I was too old to be sleeping around with "D"! She accused me as if we had made a pornography video for the world to see. No one knew for sure, it was all based on speculation and gossip. Drake and I scheduled meetings with Pastor, and he gave us individual counseling. Only Pastor, Drake, God and me, would know what had been revealed behind those closed doors. Pastor gave us his stamp of approval and set us free to continue **SINGING** and dancing to the beat of our own music! Our singing got even better as we continued ministering in music. We were the headliners that packed our church and the many other churches we were invited to.

"Cha-ching, Cha-ching Cha-ching..."

Another lesson I learned was that church is a business, anything goes. As long as there is plenty of wall to wall carpet, there will always be plenty of space to sweep things under.

The first Sunday without my sister and her family seated in the pews was very emotional for me, but I could always hear Honey's voice, whenever I came to a roadblock in my life. As a girl, when I would ask to go to church with our neighbors, she would allow me to go, but also warned me not to get too involved because I would learn that "Jesus" was a myth just like "Santa Claus" -- my heart would be broken. Honey wasn't always right, but in my world, ninety percent of the time she was. This time I'd pray extra hard that she wasn't. My heart had been broken so many times! It caused me to look for love in all the wrong places. I needed this place, the church, to be the right place for healing, not hurting...

Everyone was in their rightful places.

Drake began to sing:

See, real-life confrontations, caused our vows to break
But I learned the word forgiveness
Can in time chase the pain away
True love made our hearts inseparable
If we just believe

With tears streaming down my face but my eyes focused on Drake, I sang my verse:

I need to know, yes it's okay
Can I hurdle this storm, yes, but only together
With love in our hearts the only way
Somehow things will work out just you wait and see...

There was not a dry eye in the building on that day, and for Drake and me, this was not a performance. We were singing from our hearts.

Chapter 28

❖

Finding My Way into His Grace

D rake and I had gotten out of control. While pastor was preaching, we were making suggestive gestures at each other. He would lick his lips, and I would wink! We would go back and forth. There were even a couple times I had an outburst of laughter and tried to play it off with a cough. We were not very interested in any messages from the pastor that he thought he was trying to deliver. During the end of the sermon, Drake had to stop entertaining me and pay strict attention to his father. He was responsible for making the keyboard talk in between pastor's breaths. In addition to that, there was the 'lampshade' ladies parading around the front of the church, and a few others laid out on the floor with these huge handkerchiefs, that looked like big napkins, thrown across their knees to cover any unwanted images. I'd heard someone say they were slain in the spirit! *Really?* The last time I checked, Webster's explanation of slain meant to kill. If this meant they were killing spirits, then perhaps this was an accurate description.

"O" discreetly pointed to the ushers standing off to the side, looking as if they were playing London Bridge is Falling Down with a lady caught in between their grasp. She said, "Kay" (a nickname she'd given me as a joke after she seen "D & K" in big gold letters posted on the church bulletin board), *"Y'all are going straight to Hell in a hand basket*!!!" To this day I don't know why we were going in a hand basket. No matter how hard I laughed, deep inside it really wasn't so funny when I gave it some serious thought. *Hell, Fire and Brimstone?!* Wait a minute, our former associate pastor preached a life-changing sermon on that title. Nobody would ever forget what she taught! If there's such a place, I definitely didn't want to go! I've always understood and received "O's" messages, regardless of her sarcasm when she said them. She was the type of person that said things jokingly, but she was really serious.

I took one last look at this circus that I had allowed myself to become a part of and then looked at "O" with what she referred to as my blank stare. I had an epiphany to run as fast as I could in an effort to save my life! How ironic it was that I visited the church seeking refuge and I'd leave in worst shape than I had come. An additional fear had been imposed on my spirit -- being tormented in a place called Hell. My heart was not only broken, but it was now shattered in a million pieces.

Through all of the sermons and all of the fiascos, I had been introduced to the Savior, yet I had not been SAVED. Where was He? Did He realize that I came seeking refuge? Was He forced to turn away from my wicked ways, or was I just not worthy of being SAVED?

I know now that the Praise Tabernacle family could never teach me how to walk with the Savior. Their expertise was in teaching me how to walk (or run) further away. Again, the direction of my life had me searching for an escape.

In the midst of this circus that was going on, I held up my finger (as I had been taught), signaled to my children, and we walked out. I wanted to say something to Drake, but now just wasn't the time.

Later that evening Drake called, ready for the ole' *in - home re-hearsal routine*. We were rehearsing more frequently now. Storms were not the only thing that now prompted the late-night visits. I shared with him my feelings about being Hell bound. I just couldn't continue living like this. There was enough God inside of me to finally feel some type of conviction. Drake obviously felt nothing! He laughed and started with his same philosophy about God forgiving all who ask, regardless of how many times they repeated the same sin!! Why would I expect any more than the response he so freely gave, considering it was his father who was leading us. This was the same man who instructed us to cast our cares upon him, so he could take 'em to God. When Drake couldn't get me to listen to him, he suggested I call our pastor. Of course, that was never going to happen. This was probably not just about taking more of my business to God. More than likely, it was just an opportunity for him and Drake to sit around laughing, then cheerfully giving each other

the old high five.

I had had enough! A few weeks passed with no church and no communication from the people I had grown to love. Yet, the separation was well worth it if it meant I would not go to Hell in a handbasket. I'm sure they called, my phone would ring constantly. It was annoying, but I refused to answer it. I finally took it off the hook. I didn't want to be persuaded by Drake nor Pastor to return to the circus, and somehow I knew if I had answered, it would be a sign of weakness and I'd return.

Since I had gotten accustomed to being in church four days (and sometimes nights) a week, my children and I were bored sitting at home. I kept listening to BeeBee and CeeCee, reminisc-ing with feelings of loneliness and despair. I had started to read my Bible, something I should've been doing anyway. That book was hard to put down. It was like an autobiography of God. I was immersed in every page just like I had felt when I read the Autobiography of Malcolm X, truly a page-turner. I could hardly go to the bathroom without it.

I had begun to feel like me and God were having one on one conversations, finally a personal relationship. I would be in my room singing along with my CDs, clapping and crying, not always sad tears. I'd like to think some of my tears were cleansing me, washing away some of the guilt and shame I held inside. Having church in my room, all alone, freed me from any judgment.

Perhaps it sounded like I was having too much fun in my room with my gospel music blasting. I gained four new members. My children started joining me, and we were having a praise party of our own. One night, Onyx who has always been my little jokester, started pretending he caught the holy ghost, as he called it. He had learned the lampshade ladies holy dance to the tee. He had even learned how to mimic that gibberish as if he was speaking in an unknown language. Then out of nowhere, he started crying and really praising God. It took a minute, but once things calmed down, he asked if he could start going to church with Auntie Kyndra. I would not discourage him, it didn't matter how I had been scorned by church folks. It was me who opened the door to religion in our household. God was watching over us, and my son was a prime example of that.

Isaiah 11:6 (ESV)
The calf and the yearling will be safe with the lion and the little child will lead them all...

The following Sunday we decided to attend "The Wounded Soldiers Ministry" The parking lot was filled to capacity, but a parking attendant offered to valet park for me. ***Excuse me!,*** *They're over here doing it big!* There was also an usher who seated us. The atmosphere was warm and peaceful. The lady at the front of the church was not wearing a lampshade. She was beautiful -- all glammed up. She asked everyone to stand as she welcomed first-time visitors (*us*). Following that, they sang a welcome song, and many of the people came to hug us. Kyndra spotted us, she too gave me a squeeze so tight and whispered in my ear, *"So glad you came."* That was the greatest feeling for me to be welcomed by my big sister. This day was going perfectly. I would not tarry after the service ended. I would leave with my dignity intact. I wanted so much for her just to be proud of me.

They would get right to God's business, no long praise service, no bodyguards escorting the pastor to the podium. She just stood up in her robe, and yes, her lampshade adorned the crown of her head. She let out a powerful ***"Praise the Lord Everybody!"*** and I knew immediately that I was in for a real spiritual feast, something I hadn't been served since she left Praise Tabernacle!

There was a presence about Pastor Lilly that just couldn't be described. She commanded the room with poise and elegance. She was confident, not boastful, and you wanted to cling to every word that came out of her mouth. Somehow, without her ever saying it, you knew God was speaking through her ...

"I won't be before you long today. As I was studying on last night (she closed her eyes for a moment) God began to speak to me about 'Grace' He said, somebody needs to know His 'Grace' is sufficient for thee."

She went on to tell us a brief story of how this person was lost as a young girl and welcomed into a fast-paced life by older women who taught her how to survive and conduct herself around men. She was taught that promiscuity was ok, just be selective and get paid! Nothing is free! Pastor paused and hummed just a little. She said, *"Oh but church, I'm here to tell you that "Salvation is free!"* As she continued, she said, *"I'm gonna entitle my sermon today, 'His Grace'. I will be speaking from Ephesians 2:8; May the Lord add a blessing to the reading of His word. For by Grace you have been saved through faith. And this is not your own doing; it is the Gift of God."*

I'm telling you, it was so quiet in that church as everyone, teens included, were sniffling as they listened intently. *"I don't need to know what you're going through today because we are all going through something! I'm here to tell you church about His Grace."* As we felt her sermon coming to an end, she hummed a little, and the pianist began to play soft music, but there was no huffing and puffing as if she was going to blow the house down or have an asthma attack!

Hebrews 4:6 (ESV) *"Let us then with confidence draw near to the throne of 'Grace', that we may receive mercy and find Grace to help in our time of need.'*

Our earthy families will fail us over and over again, but our God never fails...

My head was bowed, my hands to my face with a well of tears running through my fingers. God was speaking to me through Pastor Lilly. He was always there. I was just in the wrong place, and that was hindering me from receiving Him. Now I was in the right place, and this was undoubtedly the right time. Pastor prayed, *"God is speaking to someone right now" You know who you are; He's saying not only you, but we have all fallen short of His glory. He isn't concerned with how many men you've slept with, or even the man that was married! Read the story about the woman at the well! God's no respecter of persons. His Grace, my sister, His Grace is sufficient..."*

I stood, and an usher came over to me and handed me some Kleenex, as I wiped my drenched face she led me to the altar...

Pastor opened her arms as if she was God waiting to receive me. *"Sister Kamara,"* she said, *"I know what you've been going through; I've been there too, but God sees all, and He knows all. We don't have to tell anybody our life story. We CAN go to God and cast our cares upon Him."* She prayed what she referred to as the prayer of faith over me. She thanked me for coming to visit her ministry because I could've gone somewhere else. I fell to my knees and laid at the altar. As I continued weeping, someone gave the benediction... *"We hope that the healing process has begun for you here today at The Wounded Soldiers Ministry, for it is our goal to reach as many souls through God as we can."*

As I departed that building, I hugged my children, and I squeezed Onyx just a little bit tighter. It was because of his suggestion that we visited this church today.

My soul was satisfied...

My life changed that day, instantly. I realized that I was an addict. I was addicted to men and all the lust and lies I allowed them to inject into my soul. I had found a new man, a real man, the ultimate man, *"God",* who was able to supply some of my wants and all of my needs, if I just learned to "Trust and Believe."

That wasn't our last visit to The Wounded Soldier's Ministry, and every visit was just as powerful as the first. I would always leave filled up from the presence of God as He moved through Pastor Lilly. I reminded myself this was Kyndra's place of worship and since she and I were at a comfortable place, I never wanted to jeopardize our relationship as sister's again. I would never join her church.

It's now winter and the news forecasts a Nor'easter headed our way. I didn't feel like I was running, or as I would always put it, escaping, I had an unction in my spirit that it was okay for me to move on. I felt confident now as a woman of God, strong and able to make better choices for myself and my children. I always prayed and asked God for a sign, and He would always show up (*or at least I thought it was Him*).

Barbara and I talked periodically, but when I heard her voice this time, I could hear an extra bit of excitement in her tone! First, we both shared our testimonies about this God that we were experiencing. She was a little further along in her walk than I was. She was the First Lady, and their congregation was well on the way. Hakeem, by her description, was a changed man and by way of his teachings, souls were being saved daily. I could hear the enthusiasm and sincerity in her voice. She said that they always spoke of Diamond and wanted her to be a part of their lives. She asked me to think about relocating to Georgia. She told me that I wouldn't believe the sizes of the houses there. They were nothing like Jersey houses – far bigger, better and cheaper. She then went on to say they had plenty of space for the children and me until we could get established. She asked that I give it some thought, then she laughed. Determined to convince me, she reminded me of the expected Nor'easter heading my way and down south there were sunny skies, with people strolling around in blazers, not fur coats and boots. I told her I'd call her back after I thought about it, but truthfully, I knew the minute she asked the question what my answer would be. I felt like her proposal **was the answer** -- to my prayer to move on.

As usual, I reached out to my Honey! That lady was my biggest cheerleader! She was always there to give me that push, that extra vote of confidence. Without any long, drawn-out lecture, she simply said, *"Go for it! You're young, if it doesn't work out, you can come home."*

Not the same response from Kyndra, she felt as if it was the trick of the enemy! **Satan** (Hakeem); once again, was rearing his ugly head at a time when I was doing so good spiritually. My girls, "O" and "Caz" were sad, but supportive. They both were planning trips to Georgia, and I hadn't left yet. "O" talked about sending Adongo back before Herman killed him, and "Caz" loved to travel, so, I was sure she'd come to visit before "O" would.

My Diamond was devastated, she was now in her sophomore year in high school, the time when young people are developing their most everlasting friendships. She even mentioned having a boyfriend (*even more of a reason for us to relocate*). I'm sure she hated me! I know this teenager called me everything under the sun *in her mind!* She probably thought I reached another level of crazy. Well, I'm the boss, and I'm making decisions now with God. This was going to be a great opportunity for all of us! I felt it in my spirit., **we were leaving**! My sons were just happy. We were going on a road trip, no looking back. I told them Georgia was gonna be really pretty, just like when Dorothy landed in the land of Oz.

Three days later, I called Barbara back, and told her I had taken her up on her offer; we would be on our way very soon.

I had to think quickly in an attempt to beat the storm. I called in my resignation from my job! *Who does that?* **Me.** I had a weekend long apartment sale. I called Nick to let him know we were moving out of the state. Didn't think it mattered, his drive-byes were far and few between; yet he had an attitude! Malcolm and I didn't talk at all. We had since gained an everlasting bond with his daughter, Emerald. I let her know we were leaving. I knew she would relay the message to her dad. She was devastated and cried uncontrollably because I would be taking her little cry baby brother away; but I vowed we'd stay in touch.

Gas tank full (✓)

trunk packed to capacity (✓)

important papers for enrolling the children into school (✓)

Blankets, pillows and Kleenex for Diamond who's balling her eyes out (✓)

My Bible (✓)

Now one last phone call before I leave...

Me: *"Drake? I'm leaving."*

Drake: *"Leaving, going where?"*

Me: *"To Georgia."*

Drake: *"Huh? What are you talking about?"*

Me: *"I'm all packed and ready to take this 14-hour drive, relocating to Georgia."*

Drake: *"But, I've been meaning to call you. I haven't been feeling like myself lately. I've been really tired no matter how much sleep I get, my father said...(**Dial tone**)* I hung up on him before he finished that statement. I knew where he was going. If that were true, it would still be true once I arrived in the peach state.

I prayed to God for a safe journey for me and my babies. I prayed that I'd heard **His** voice and His voice alone, trusting that this would be the best decision of our lives. I thanked Him for His forgiveness of all my sins, and most importantly, I thanked Him for His Grace and Mercy.

Epilogue

Just like the lotus we too have the ability to rise from the mud, bloom out of the darkness and radiate into the world. - Unknown

Finding the path out of the gutter is not as easy for humans as it seems to be for the Lotus Flower. The waters get muddier and muddier, clouding the visibility continuously along the way, the path becoming sometimes harder to maneuver, but not impossible.

Behind every life challenge is a lesson learned, and a new purpose for living. Just know that what won't kill you, will certainly make you stronger. God only knows what the future holds. He is the only one who gives the strength and courage to go beyond. There is a desire for long-term security that is connected with the true worship of God. Kamara's journey is just beginning.

❖

About The Author

J. RENÉE

J. Renée is a writer, a healthcare worker, and an independent sales consultant. She lives her life with so much zeal and passion – first for her family, as a mother, grandmother and great grandmother, then for humankind.

Her hopes are to become a renowned author and motivational speaker, encouraging and uplifting audiences around the world, with a primary focus on young women. Her desire is to help women avoid looking for love in all the wrong places, as she has done. From her own pitfalls, she knows that with the proper guidance and self-love, women will learn not to land in the gutter in search of love.

J. Renée views her life like the "Lotus Flower" which symbolizes the purity of the heart and mind. Despite her life's many dark and gritty experiences, she has been able to take bloom with remarkable beauty, transforming many times over because of the strength and revelations she receives from God, family, and her lifelong, and loyal friends.

Contact Information

For Book signings &
Motivational Speaking Engagements call: (470) 207-1906
Email Address: Jreneejewels143@gmail.com
Instagram: www.instagram.com/jrenee143
Website: www.lifezanopenbook.com

Graphic Arts Designs and Photographs by Justin Johnson
www.instagram.com/ingeniusart
www.theingeniusart.com

www.ingramcontent.com/pod-product-compliance
Lightning Source LLC
Chambersburg PA
CBHW032121020726
47494CB00007BA/2174